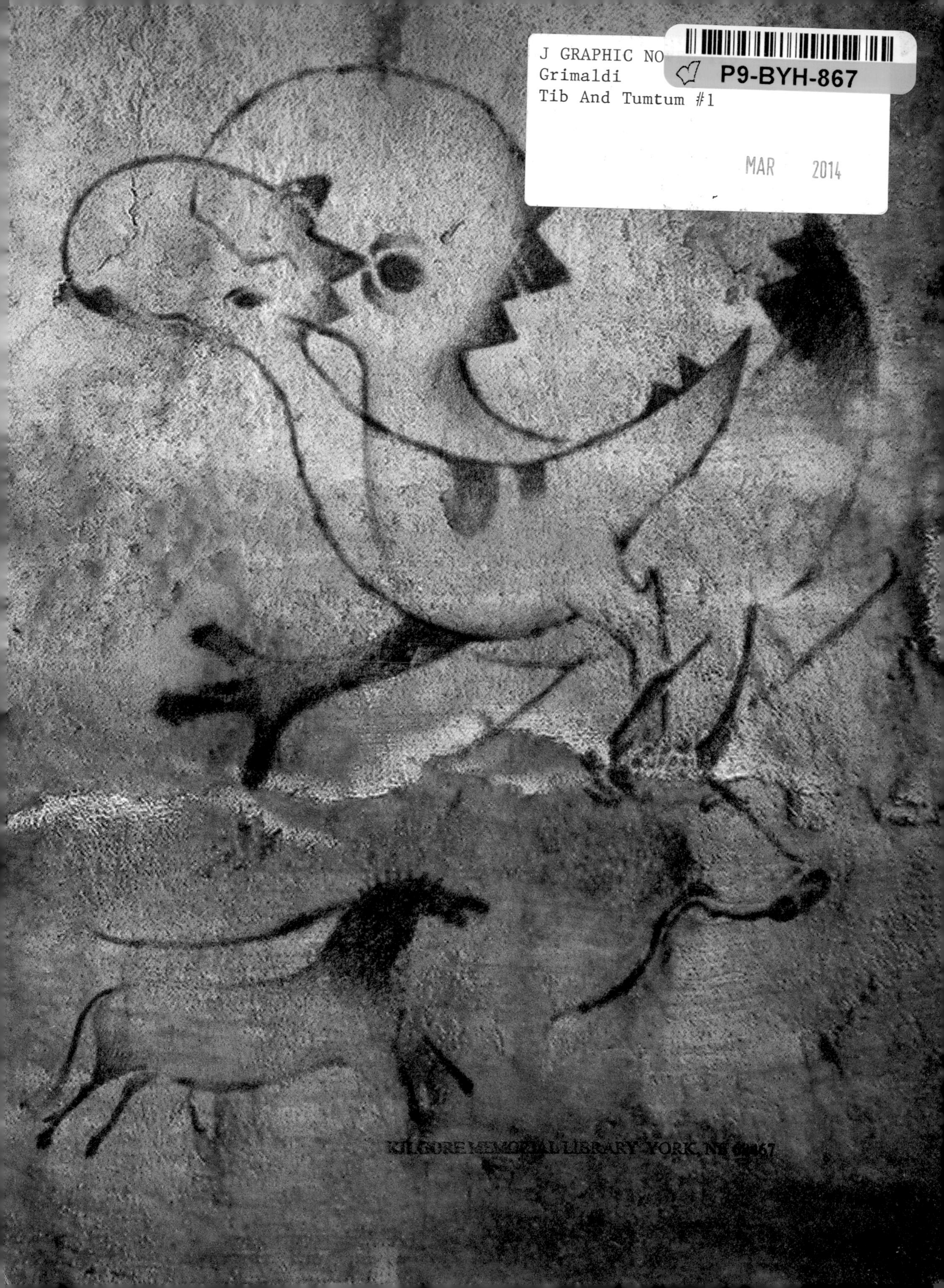

Tib & Tumtum #1

Welcome to the Tribe!

story
Grimaldi

art
Bannister

colors
Grimaldi

Graphic Universe™ · Minneapolis

To my mother Marie-Cécile, my grandmother Louise,
and my aunts Dominique and Catherine.
Thank you to my friends Elsa and Angélique, the queens of coloring.
And thanks to Fred for the Mac
—Grimaldi

Thank you to Christophe Bertschy and Fabien Vehlmann
—Bannister

Story by Grimaldi
Art by Bannister
Coloring by Grimaldi

Translation by Carol Klio Burrell

First American edition published in 2013 by Graphic Universe™.

Bienvenue au clan! by Grimaldi & Bannister © 2011—Glénat Editions
Copyright © 2013 by Lerner Publishing Group, Inc., for the US edition

Graphic Universe™ is a trademark of Lerner Publishing Group, Inc.

Graphic Universe™
A division of Lerner Publishing Group, Inc.
241 First Avenue North
Minneapolis, MN 55401 U.S.A.

Website address: www.lernerbooks.com

Library of Congress Cataloging-in-Publication Data

Grimaldi, 1975–
    [Bienvenue au clan! English.]
    Welcome to the tribe! / by Grimaldi ; illustrated by Bannister. — First American edition.
        p.   cm. — (Tib & Tumtum ; #1)
    Originally published in French in Grenoble, France, in 2011 by Glénat under the title: Bienvenue au clan!
    Summary: In a prehistoric era, Tib, a boy who is made fun of for his birthmark and his clumsiness,
makes friends with Tumtum, a big, playful red dinosaur only he ever sees. When Tumtum saves the tribe's
kids from a pack of hungry wolves, the shaman decides it's time to welcome a dinosaur into the tribe.
    ISBN 978-1-4677-1297-2 (lib. bdg. : alk. paper)
    ISBN 978-1-4677-1656-7 (eBook)
    1. Graphic novels. [1. Graphic novels. 2. Prehistoric peoples—Fiction. 3. Dinosaurs—Fiction.
4. Birthmarks—Fiction.] I. Bannister, illustrator. II. Title.
PZ7.7.6758We 2013
741.5'944—dc23   2012047639

Manufactured in the United States of America
1 – BP – 7/15/13

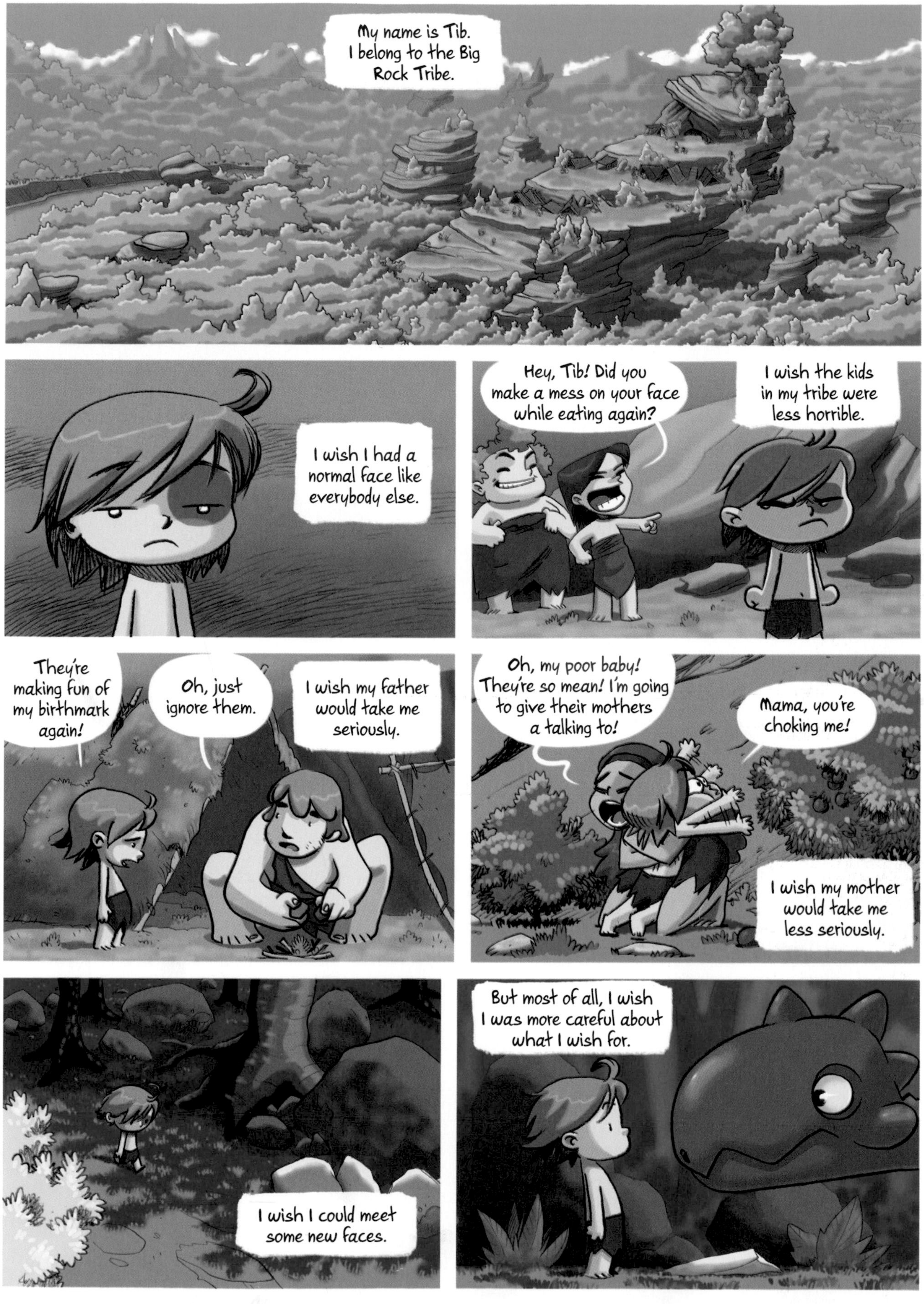
My name is Tib.
I belong to the Big Rock Tribe.
I wish I had a normal face like everybody else.
Hey, Tib! Did you make a mess on your face while eating again?
I wish the kids in my tribe were less horrible.
They're making fun of my birthmark again!
Oh, just ignore them.
I wish my father would take me seriously.
Oh, my poor baby! They're so mean! I'm going to give their mothers a talking to!
Mama, you're choking me!
I wish my mother would take me less seriously.
I wish I could meet some new faces.
But most of all, I wish I was more careful about what I wish for.

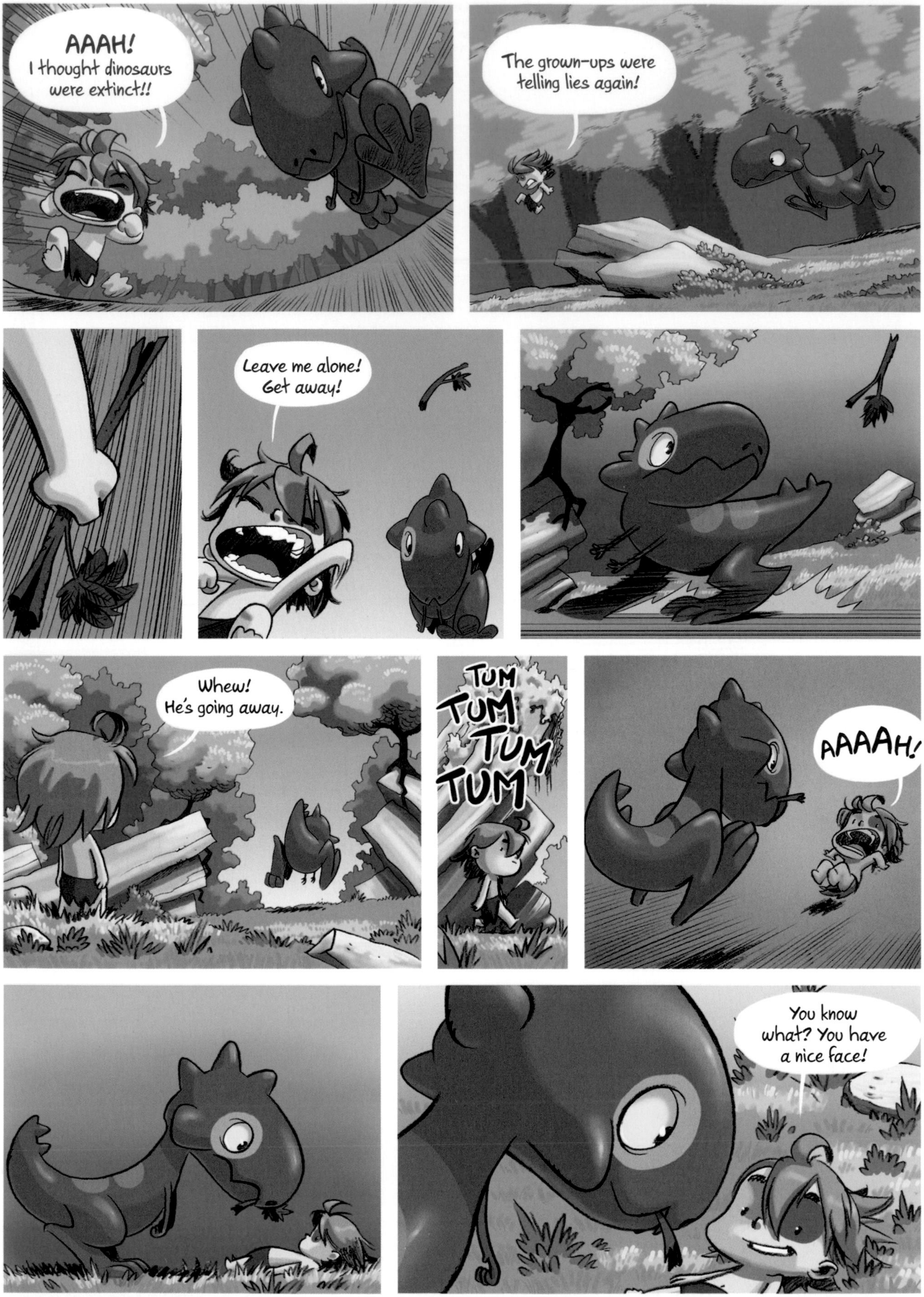
AAAH!
I thought dinosaurs were extinct!!
The grown-ups were telling lies again!
Leave me alone! Get away!
Whew! He's going away.
TUM TUM TUM TUM
AAAAH!
You know what? You have a nice face!

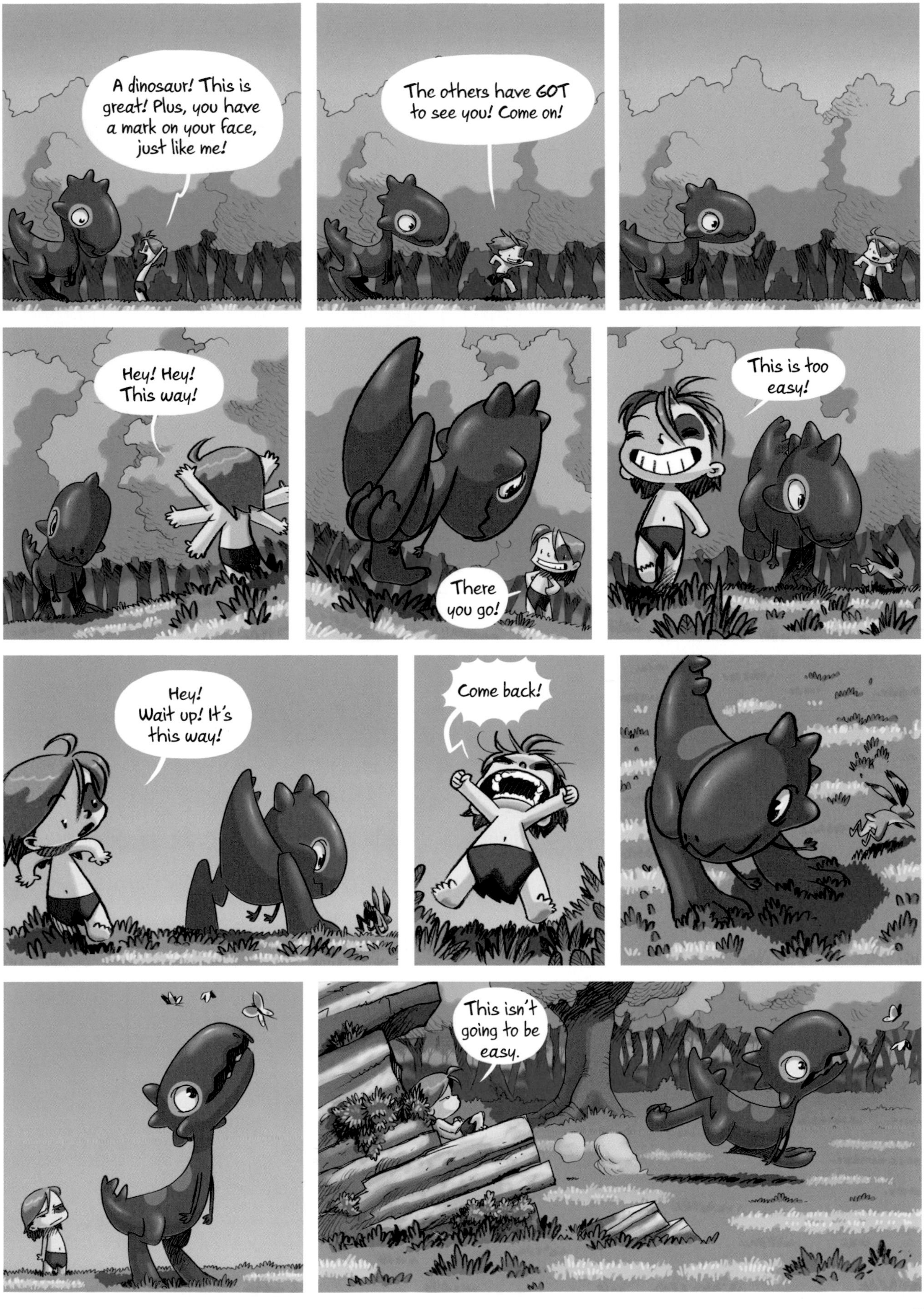
A dinosaur! This is great! Plus, you have a mark on your face, just like me!
The others have GOT to see you! Come on!
Hey! Hey! This way!
There you go!
This is too easy!
Hey! Wait up! It's this way!
Come back!
This isn't going to be easy.

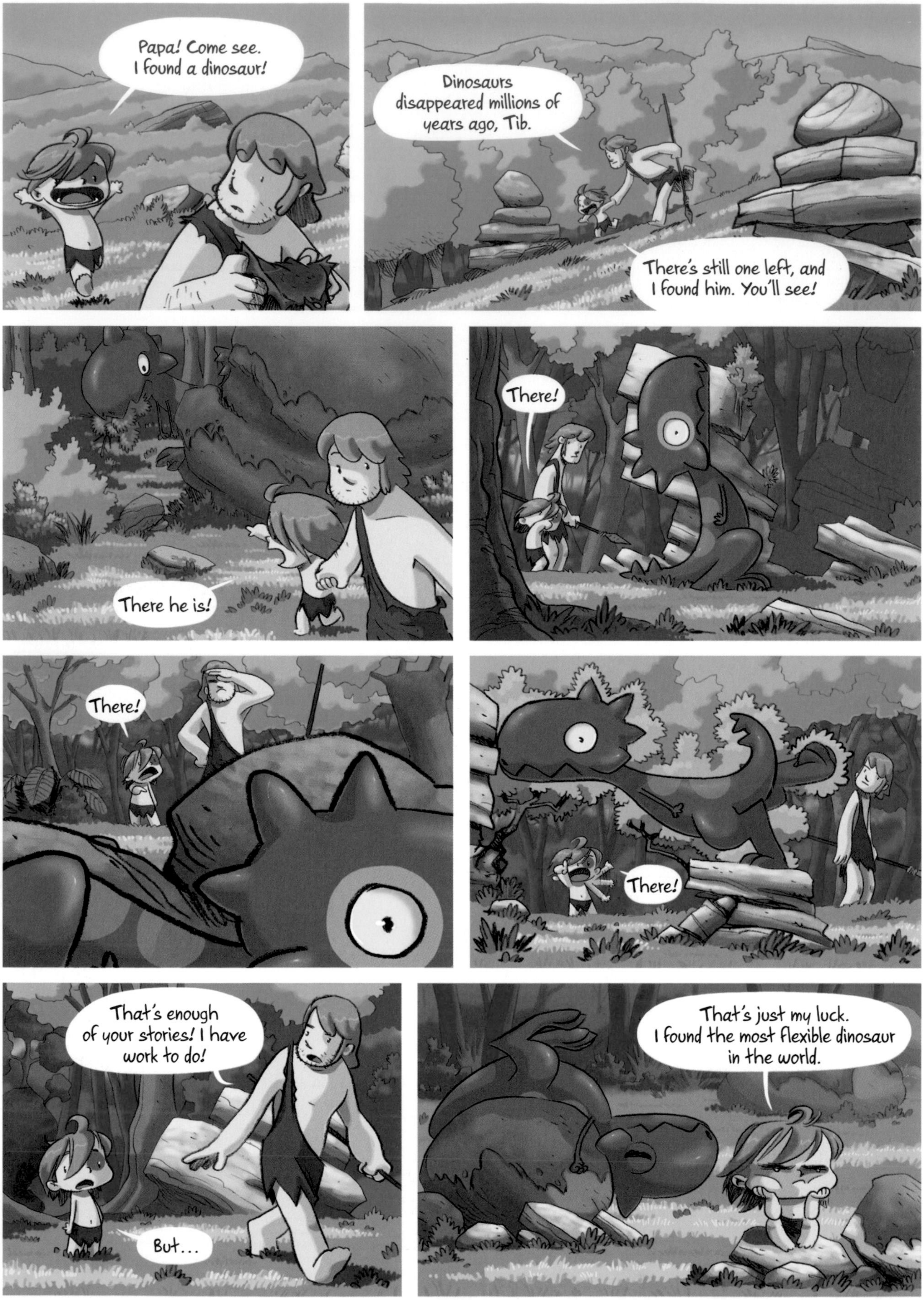
Papa! Come see. I found a dinosaur!
Dinosaurs disappeared millions of years ago, Tib.
There's still one left, and I found him. You'll see!
There he is!
There!
There!
There!
That's enough of your stories! I have work to do!
But...
That's just my luck. I found the most flexible dinosaur in the world.

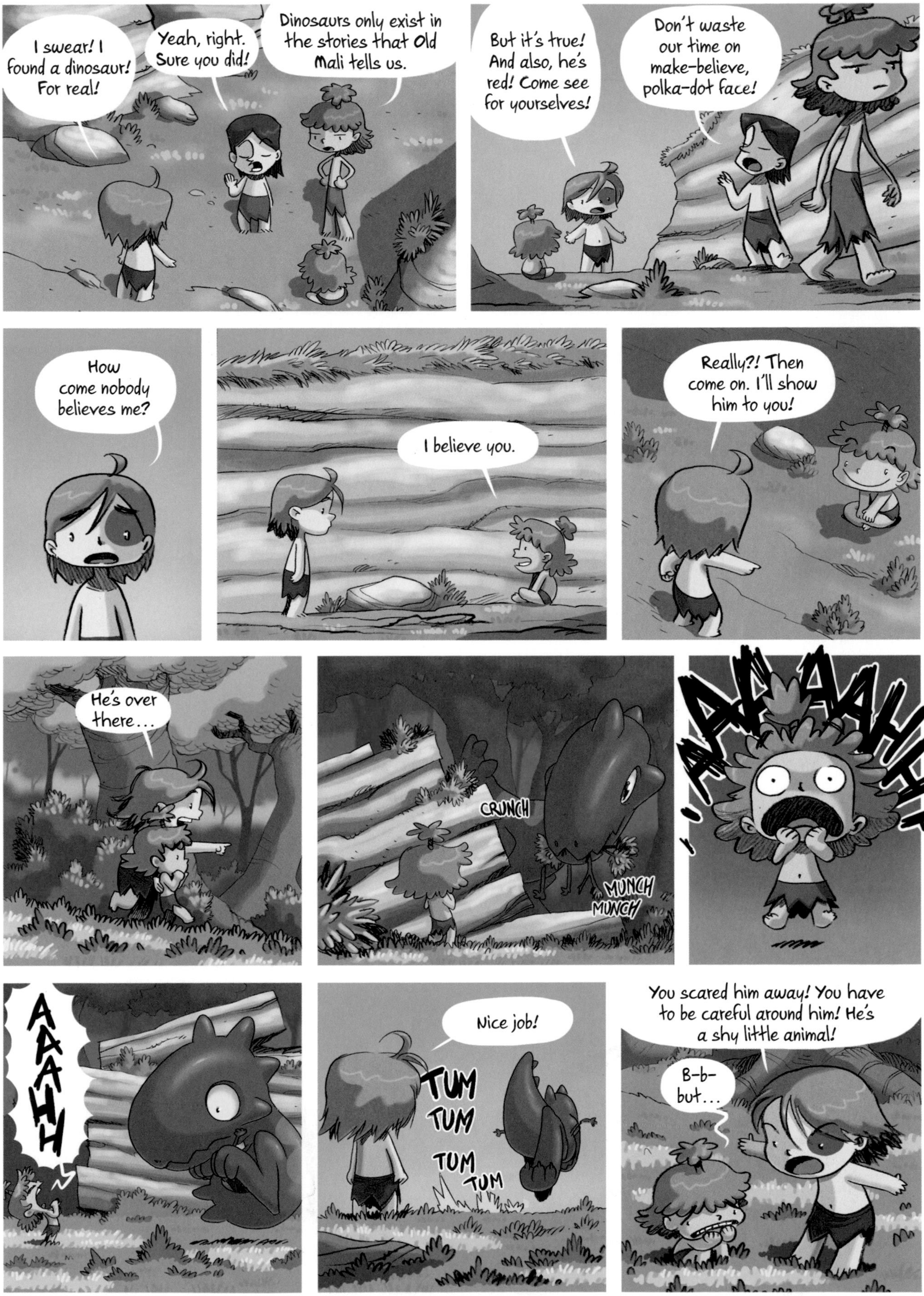
I swear! I found a dinosaur! For real!
Yeah, right. Sure you did!
Dinosaurs only exist in the stories that Old Mali tells us.
But it's true! And also, he's red! Come see for yourselves!
Don't waste our time on make-believe, polka-dot face!
How come nobody believes me?
I believe you.
Really?! Then come on. I'll show him to you!
He's over there…
CRUNCH
MUNCH MUNCH
AAAAAHH!
AAAHH
Nice job!
TUM TUM
TUM TUM
You scared him away! You have to be careful around him! He's a shy little animal!
B-b-but…

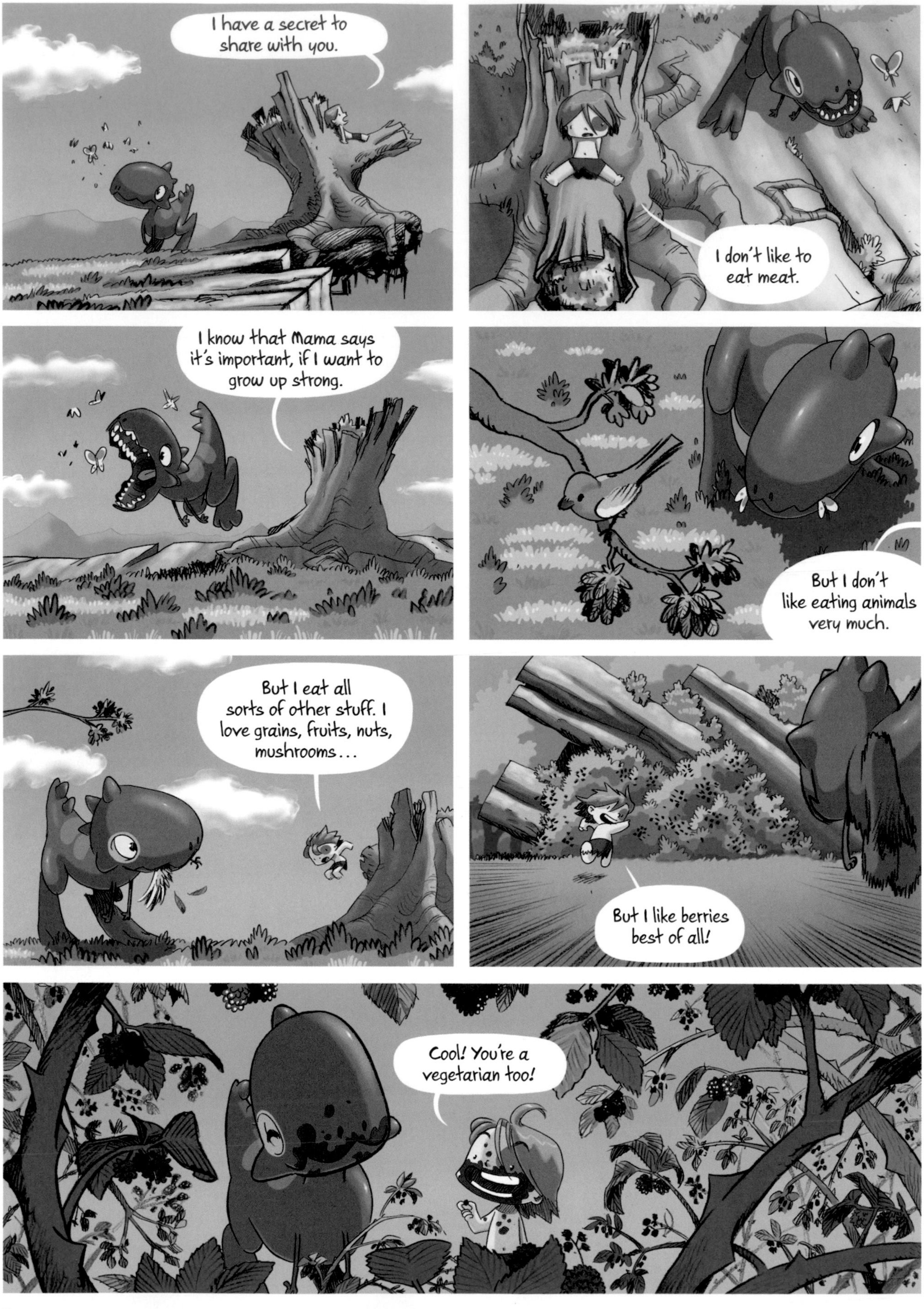
I have a secret to share with you.
I don't like to eat meat.
I know that Mama says it's important, if I want to grow up strong.
But I don't like eating animals very much.
But I eat all sorts of other stuff. I love grains, fruits, nuts, mushrooms...
But I like berries best of all!
Cool! You're a vegetarian too!

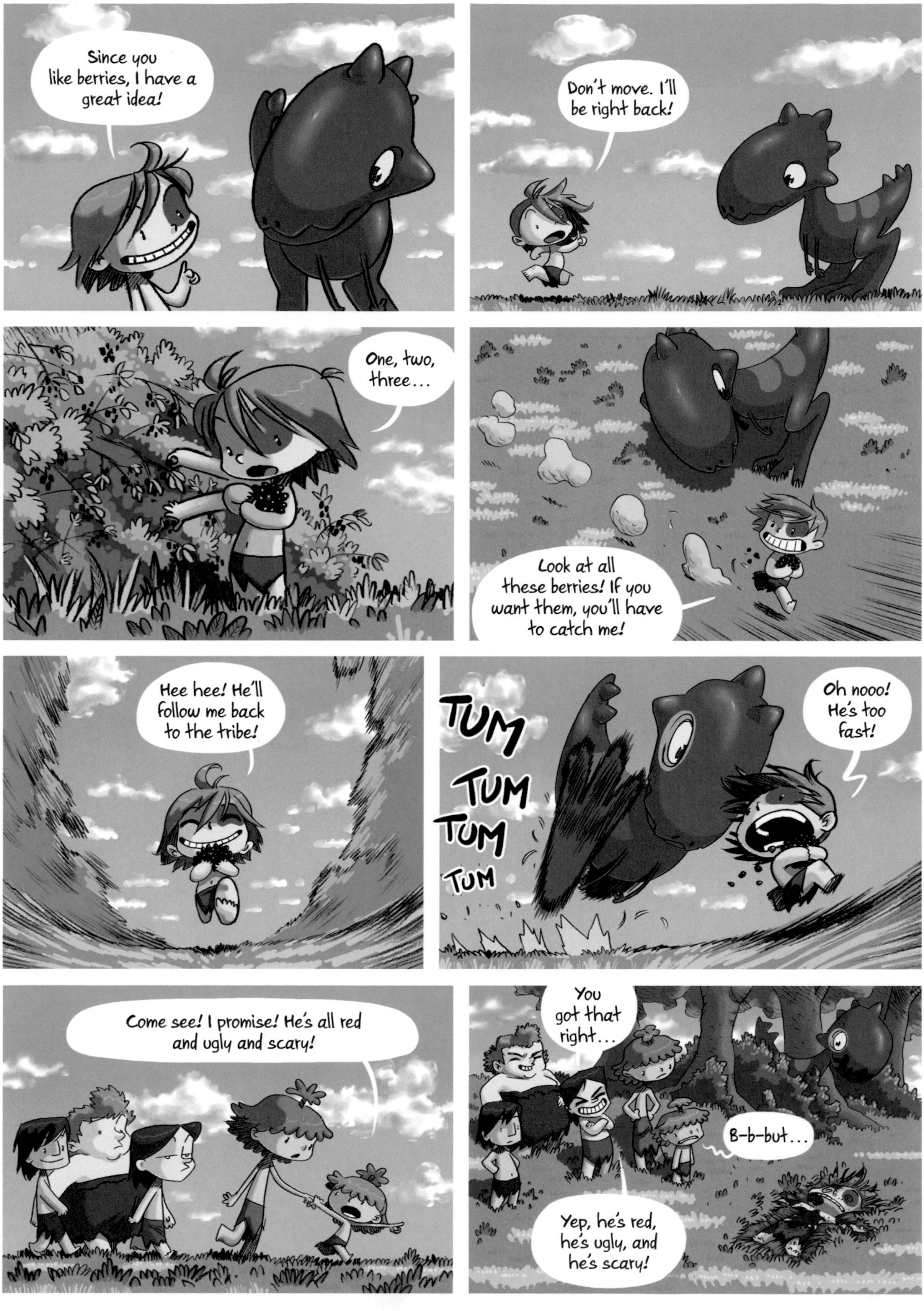
Since you like berries, I have a great idea!
Don't move. I'll be right back!
One, two, three...
Look at all these berries! If you want them, you'll have to catch me!
Hee hee! He'll follow me back to the tribe!
TUM
TUM
TUM
TUM
Oh nooo! He's too fast!
Come see! I promise! He's all red and ugly and scary!
You got that right...
B-b-but...
Yep, he's red, he's ugly, and he's scary!

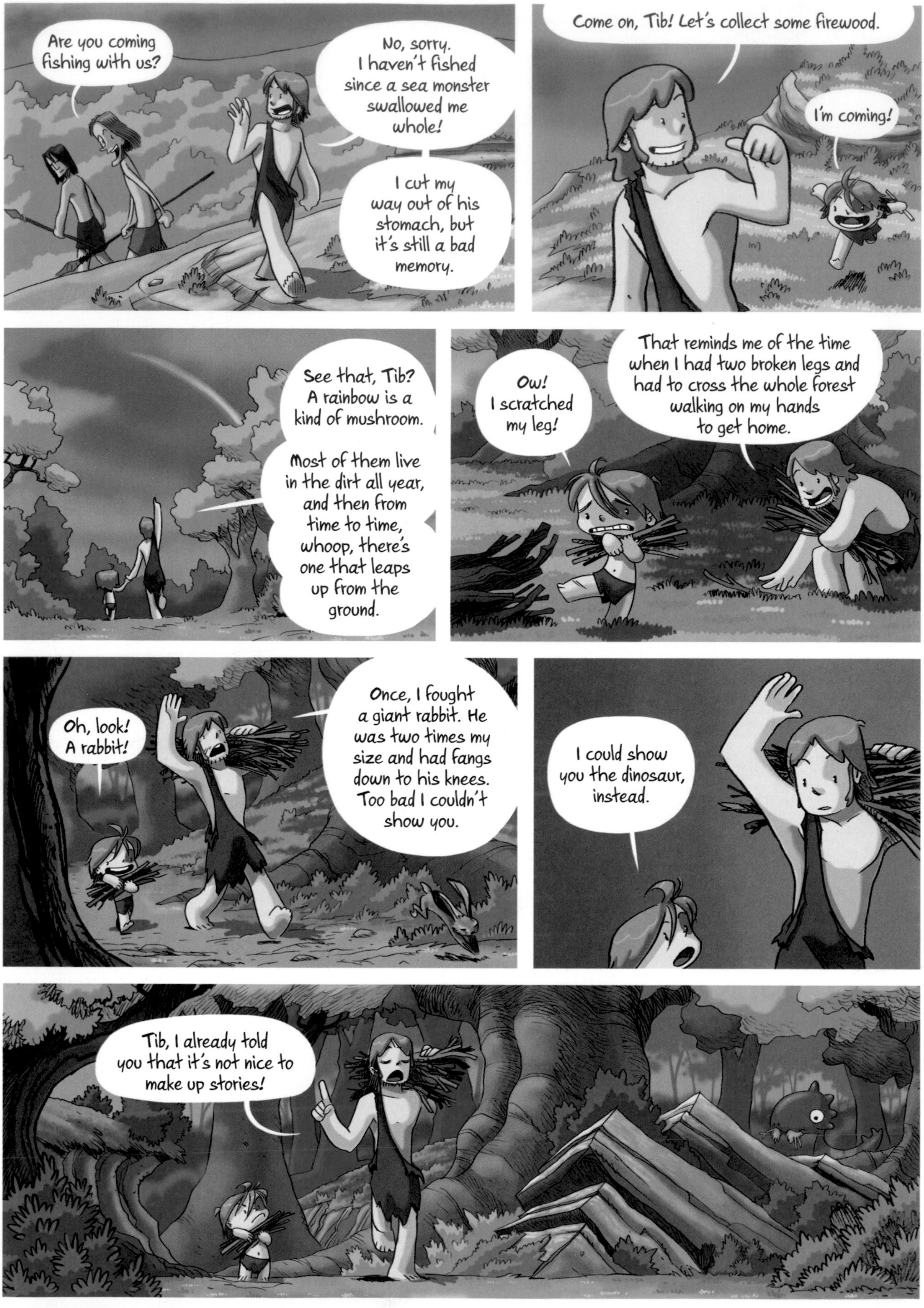

Are you coming fishing with us?
No, sorry. I haven't fished since a sea monster swallowed me whole!
I cut my way out of his stomach, but it's still a bad memory.
Come on, Tib! Let's collect some firewood.
I'm coming!
See that, Tib? A rainbow is a kind of mushroom.
Most of them live in the dirt all year, and then from time to time, whoop, there's one that leaps up from the ground.
Ow! I scratched my leg!
That reminds me of the time when I had two broken legs and had to cross the whole forest walking on my hands to get home.
Oh, look! A rabbit!
Once, I fought a giant rabbit. He was two times my size and had fangs down to his knees. Too bad I couldn't show you.
I could show you the dinosaur, instead.
Tib, I already told you that it's not nice to make up stories!

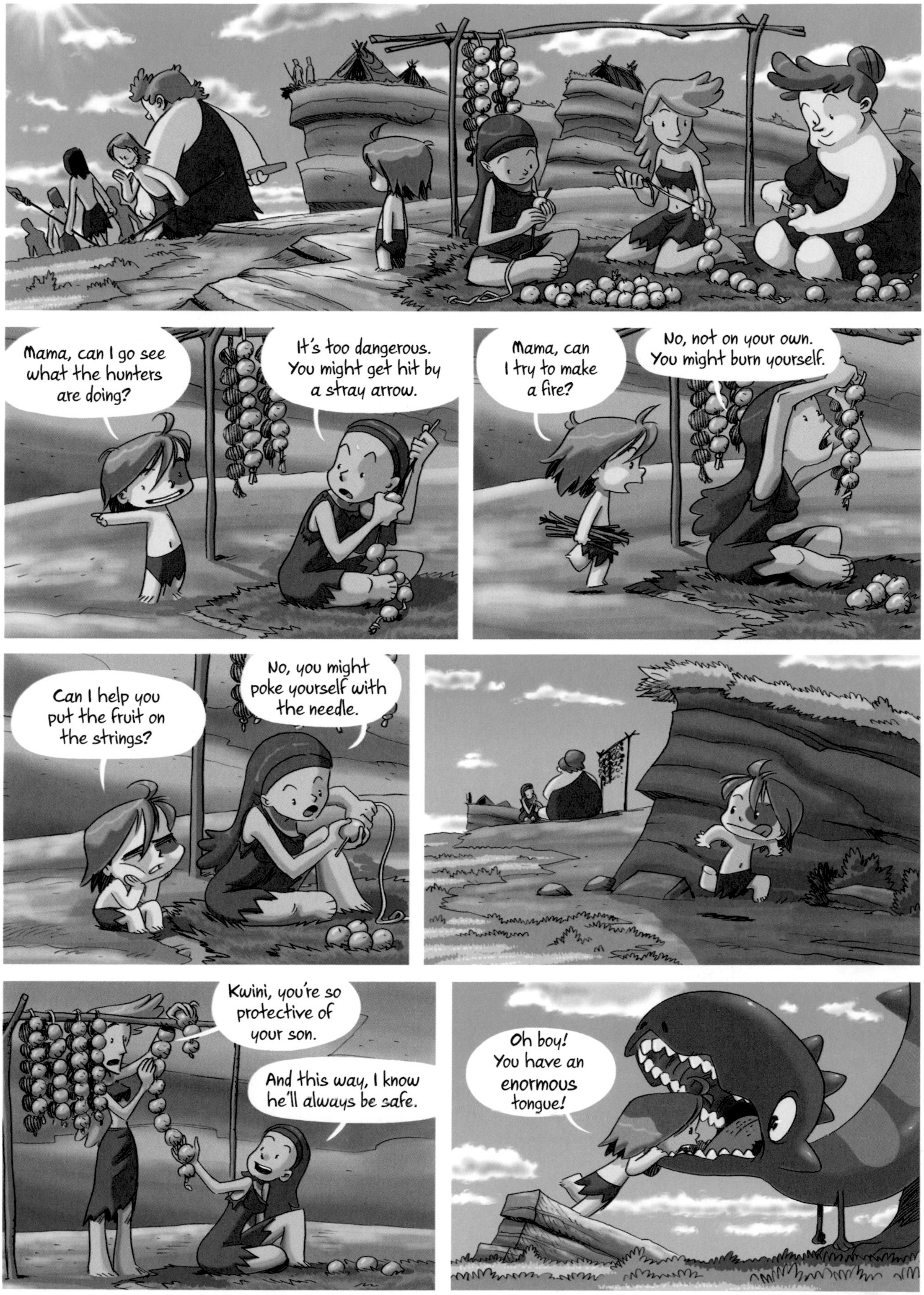
Mama, can I go see what the hunters are doing?
It's too dangerous. You might get hit by a stray arrow.
Mama, can I try to make a fire?
No, not on your own. You might burn yourself.
Can I help you put the fruit on the strings?
No, you might poke yourself with the needle.
Kwini, you're so protective of your son.
And this way, I know he'll always be safe.
Oh boy! You have an enormous tongue!

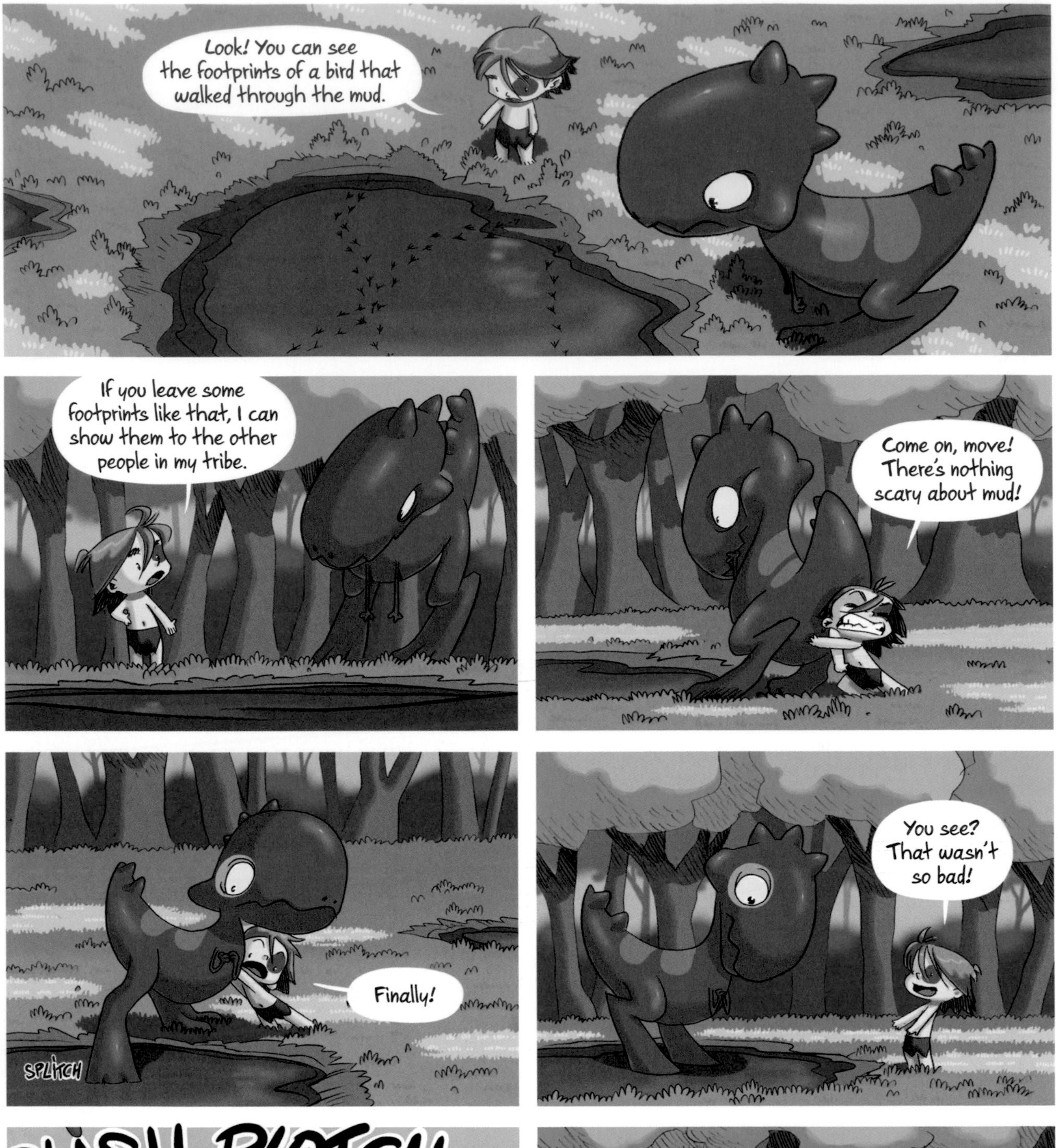
Look! You can see the footprints of a bird that walked through the mud.
If you leave some footprints like that, I can show them to the other people in my tribe.
Come on, move! There's nothing scary about mud!
SPLITCH
Finally!
You see? That wasn't so bad!
PLASH PLOTCH
This seemed like such a good idea at first...

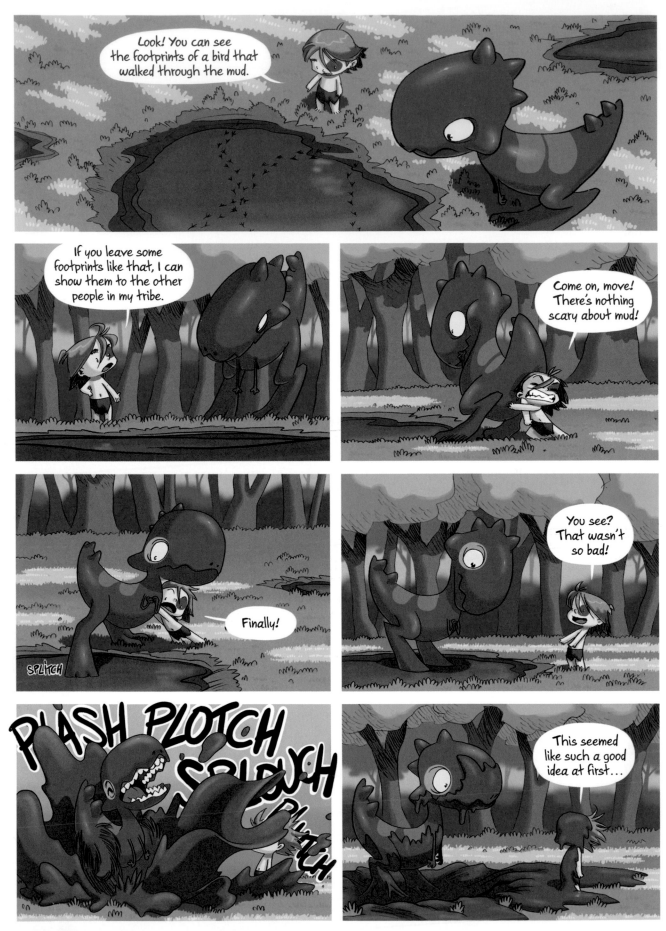

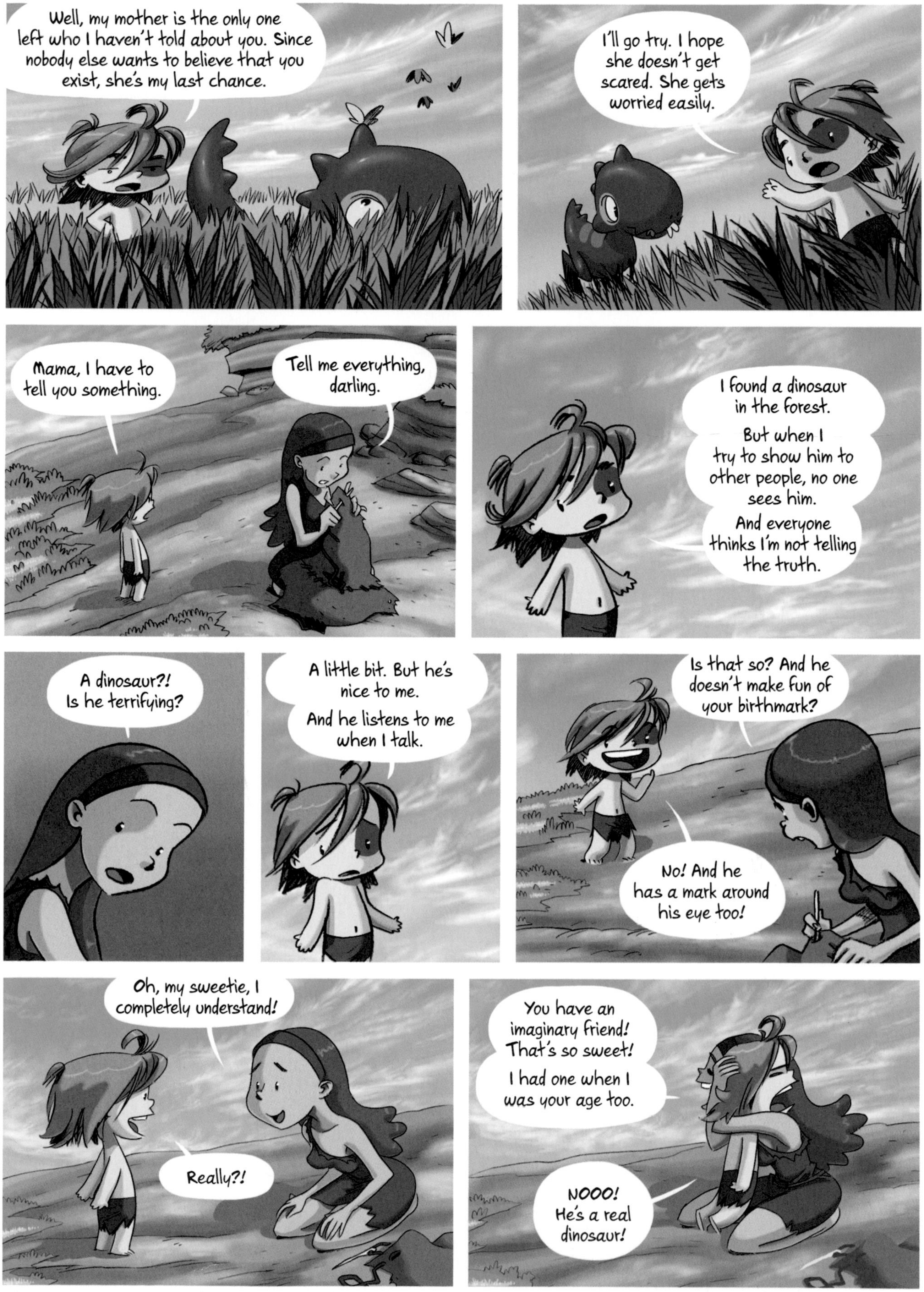

Well, my mother is the only one left who I haven't told about you. Since nobody else wants to believe that you exist, she's my last chance.
I'll go try. I hope she doesn't get scared. She gets worried easily.
Mama, I have to tell you something.
Tell me everything, darling.
I found a dinosaur in the forest.
But when I try to show him to other people, no one sees him.
And everyone thinks I'm not telling the truth.
A dinosaur?! Is he terrifying?
A little bit. But he's nice to me.
And he listens to me when I talk.
Is that so? And he doesn't make fun of your birthmark?
No! And he has a mark around his eye too!
Oh, my sweetie, I completely understand!
Really?!
You have an imaginary friend! That's so sweet!
I had one when I was your age too.
NOOO! He's a real dinosaur!

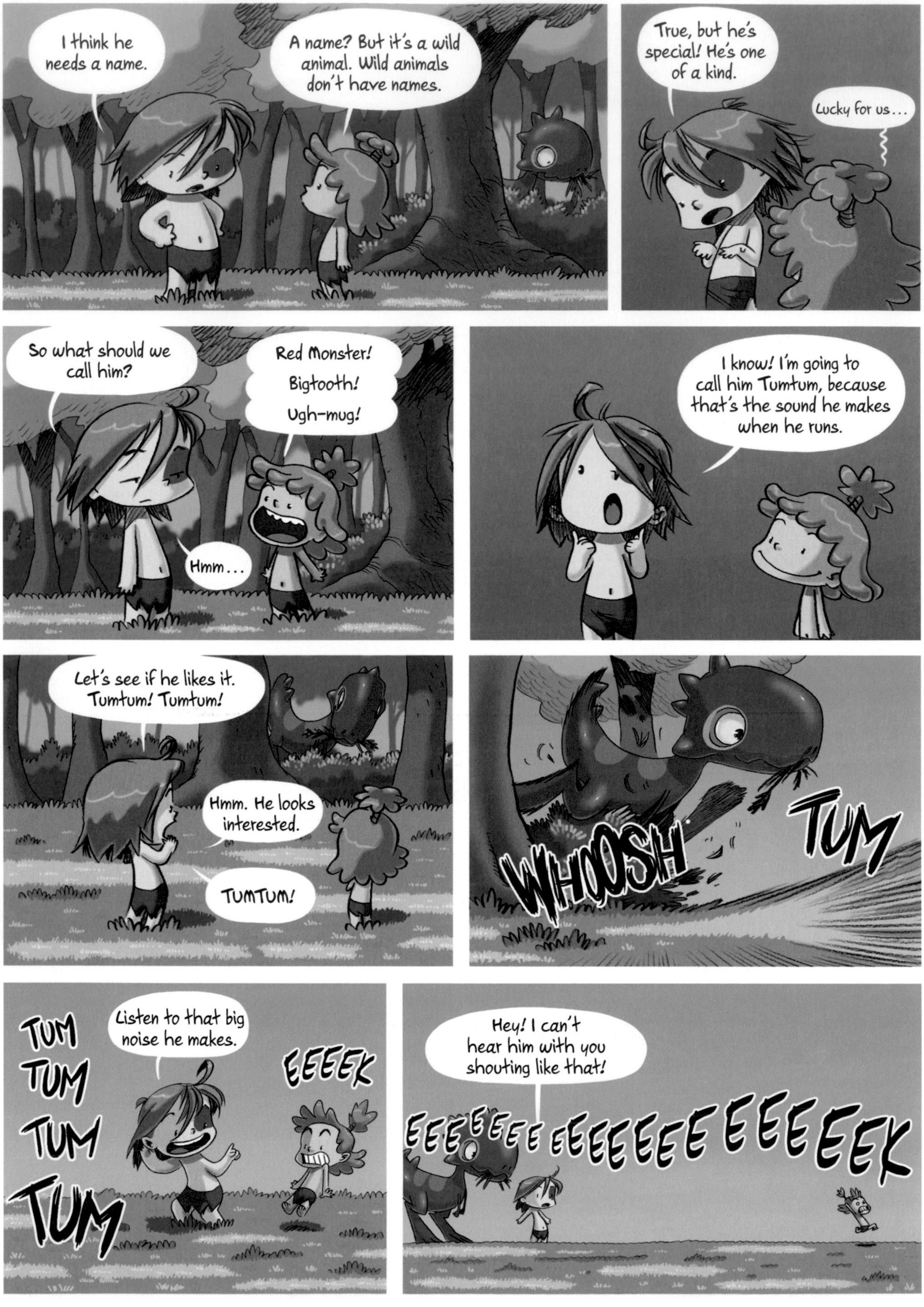
I think he needs a name.
A name? But it's a wild animal. Wild animals don't have names.
True, but he's special! He's one of a kind.
Lucky for us...
So what should we call him?
Red Monster!
Bigtooth!
Ugh-mug!
Hmm...
I know! I'm going to call him Tumtum, because that's the sound he makes when he runs.
Let's see if he likes it. Tumtum! Tumtum!
Hmm. He looks interested.
TUMTUM!
WHOOSH
TUM
TUM
TUM
TUM
TUM
Listen to that big noise he makes.
EEEEK
Hey! I can't hear him with you shouting like that!
EEEEEEEEEEEEEEEEEEEEEK

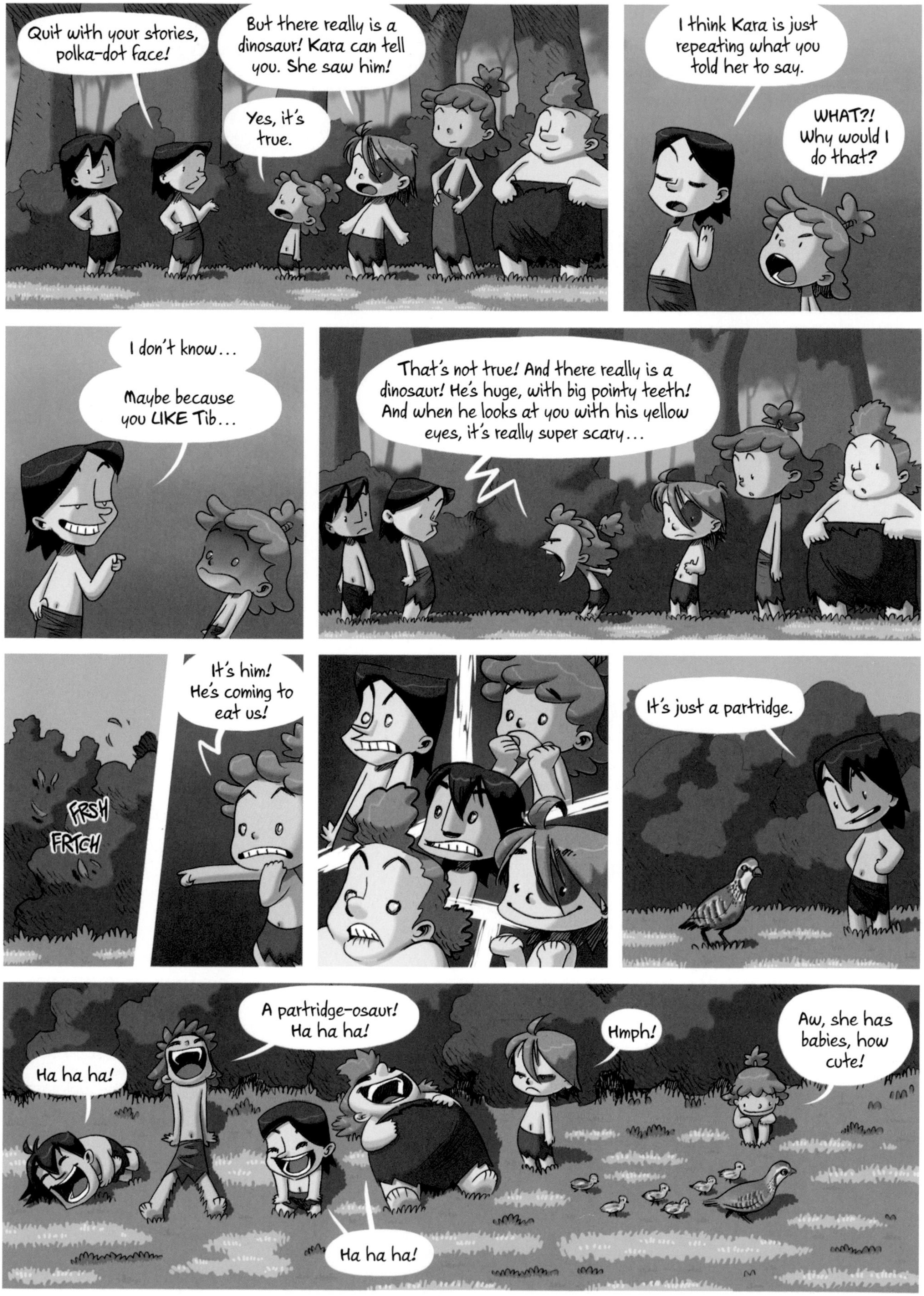
Quit with your stories, polka-dot face!
But there really is a dinosaur! Kara can tell you. She saw him!
Yes, it's true.
I think Kara is just repeating what you told her to say.
WHAT?! Why would I do that?
I don't know...
Maybe because you LIKE Tib...
That's not true! And there really is a dinosaur! He's huge, with big pointy teeth! And when he looks at you with his yellow eyes, it's really super scary...
FRSH
FRTCH
It's him! He's coming to eat us!
It's just a partridge.
Ha ha ha!
A partridge-osaur! Ha ha ha!
Hmph!
Aw, she has babies, how cute!
Ha ha ha!

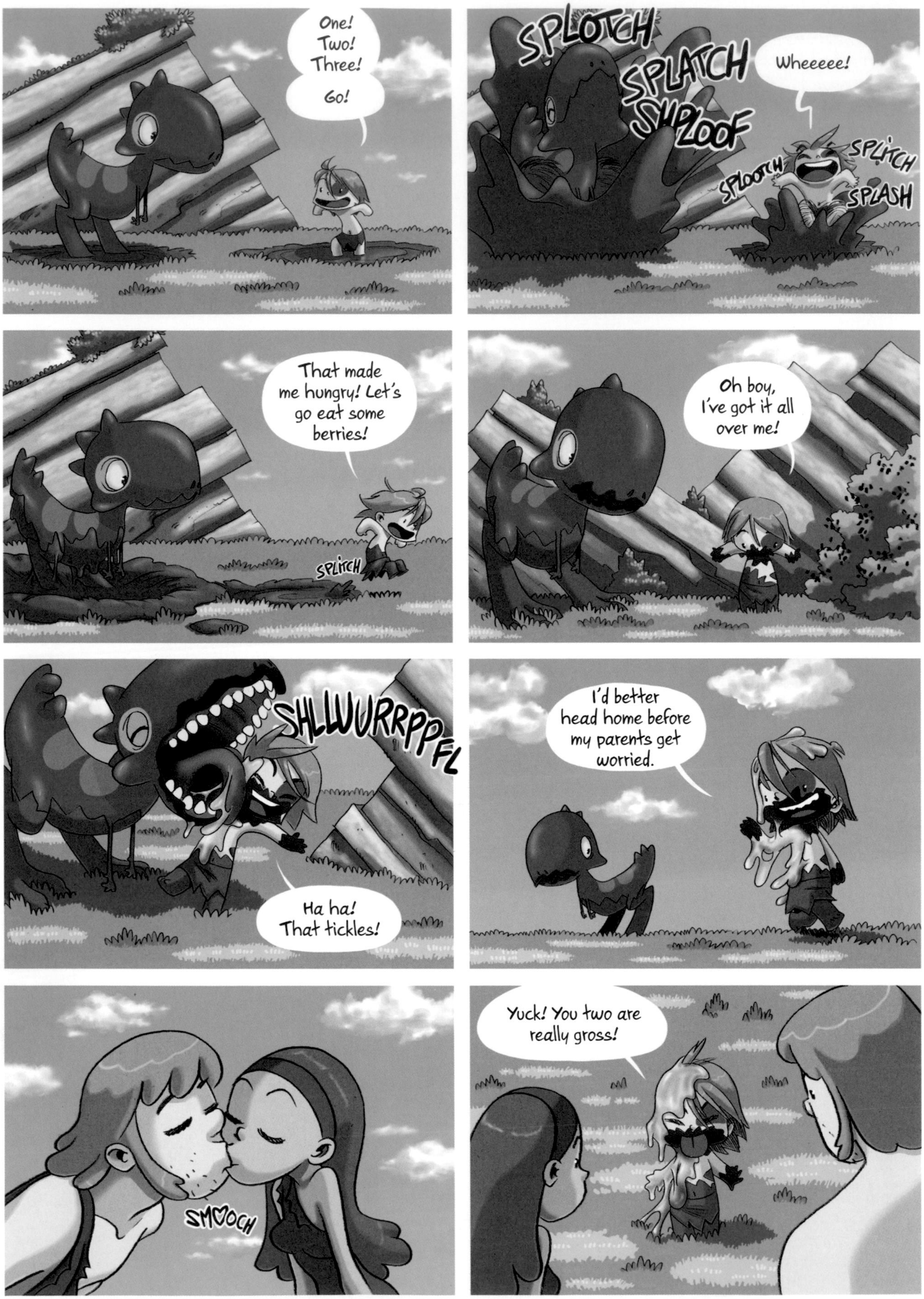
One!
Two!
Three!
Go!
SPLOTCH
SPLATCH
SHPLOOF
Wheeeee!
SPLOOTCH
SPLITCH
SPLASH
That made me hungry! Let's go eat some berries!
SPLITCH
Oh boy, I've got it all over me!
SHLUURRPPFL
Ha ha! That tickles!
I'd better head home before my parents get worried.
SMOOCH
Yuck! You two are really gross!

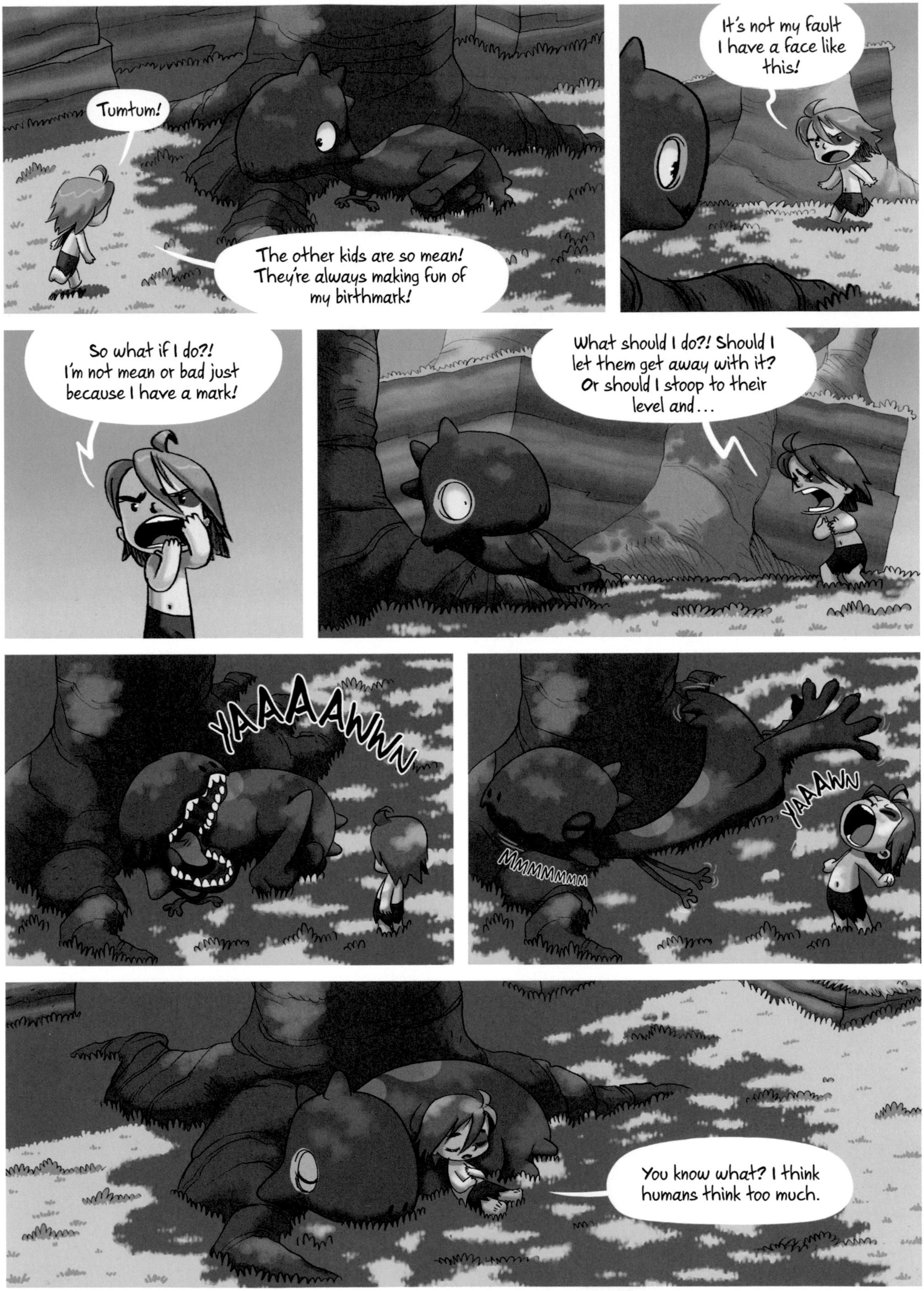
Tumtum!
The other kids are so mean! They're always making fun of my birthmark!
It's not my fault I have a face like this!
So what if I do?! I'm not mean or bad just because I have a mark!
What should I do?! Should I let them get away with it? Or should I stoop to their level and...
YAAAAWWN
MMMMMMM
YAAAWN
You know what? I think humans think too much.

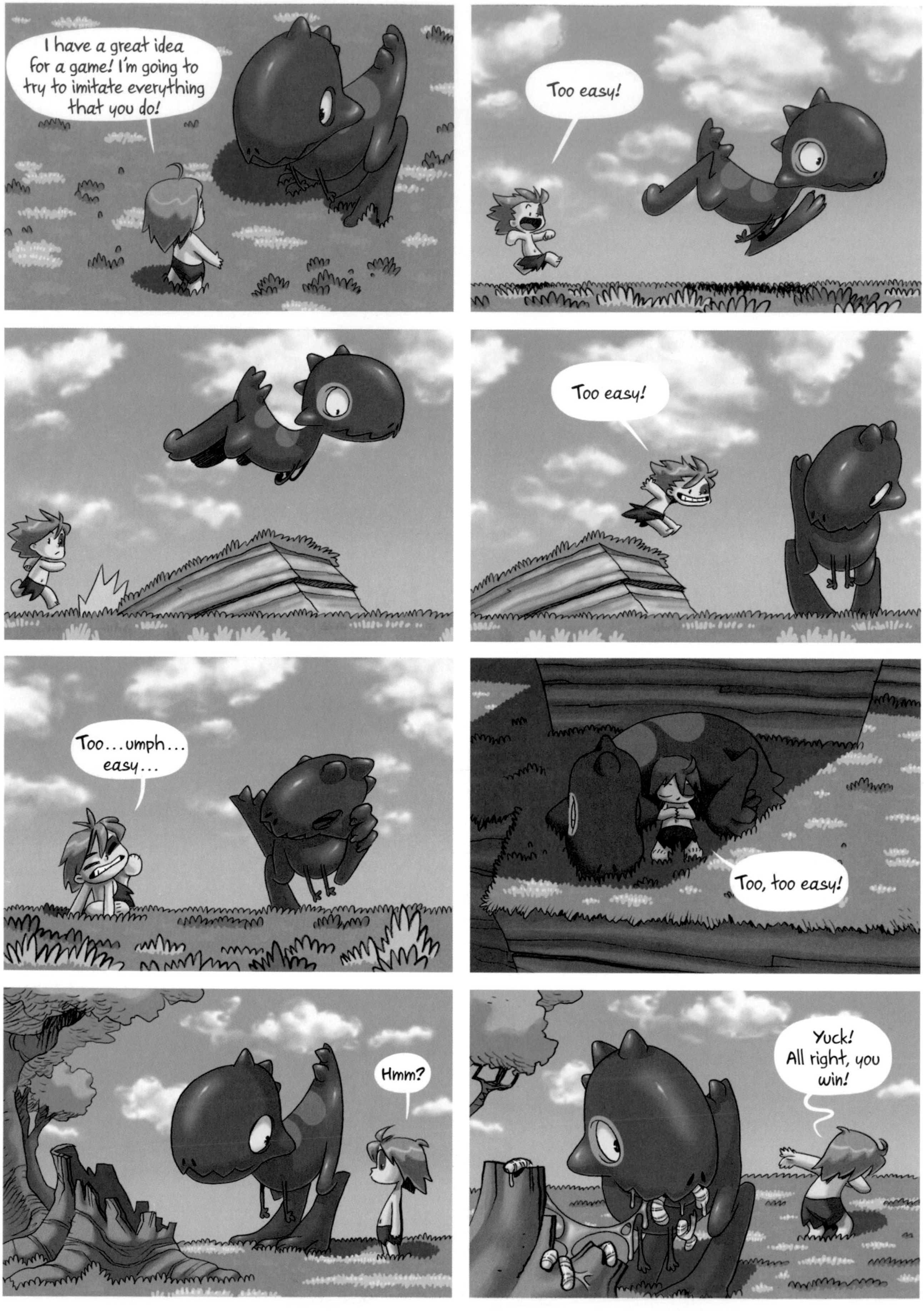
I have a great idea for a game! I'm going to try to imitate everything that you do!
Too easy!
Too easy!
Too... umph... easy...
Too, too easy!
Hmm?
Yuck! All right, you win!

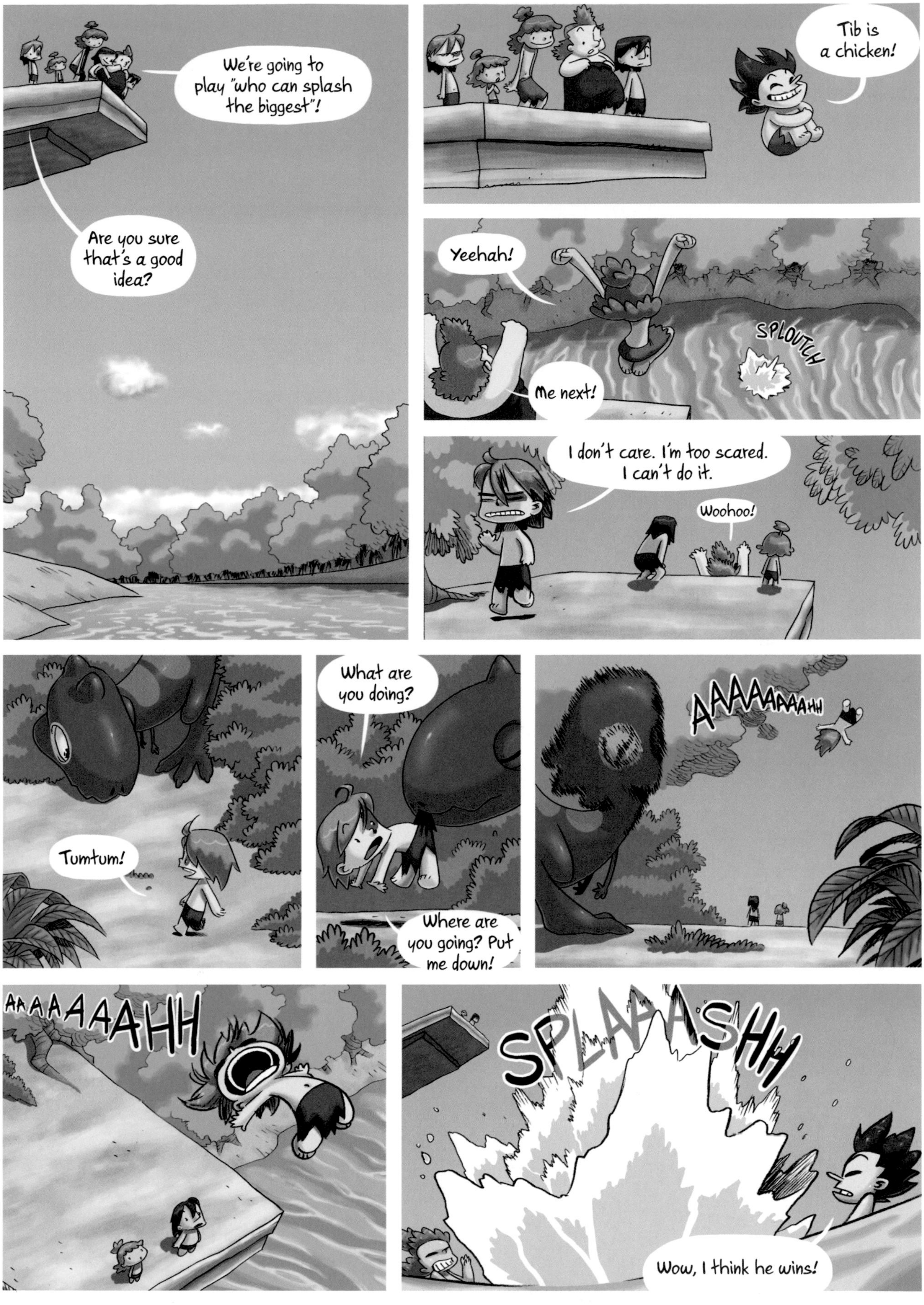
We're going to play "who can splash the biggest"!
Are you sure that's a good idea?
Tib is a chicken!
Yeehah!
SPLOUTCH
Me next!
I don't care. I'm too scared. I can't do it.
Woohoo!
Tumtum!
What are you doing?
Where are you going? Put me down!
AAAAAAAAHH
AAAAAAAHH
SPLAAASHH
Wow, I think he wins!

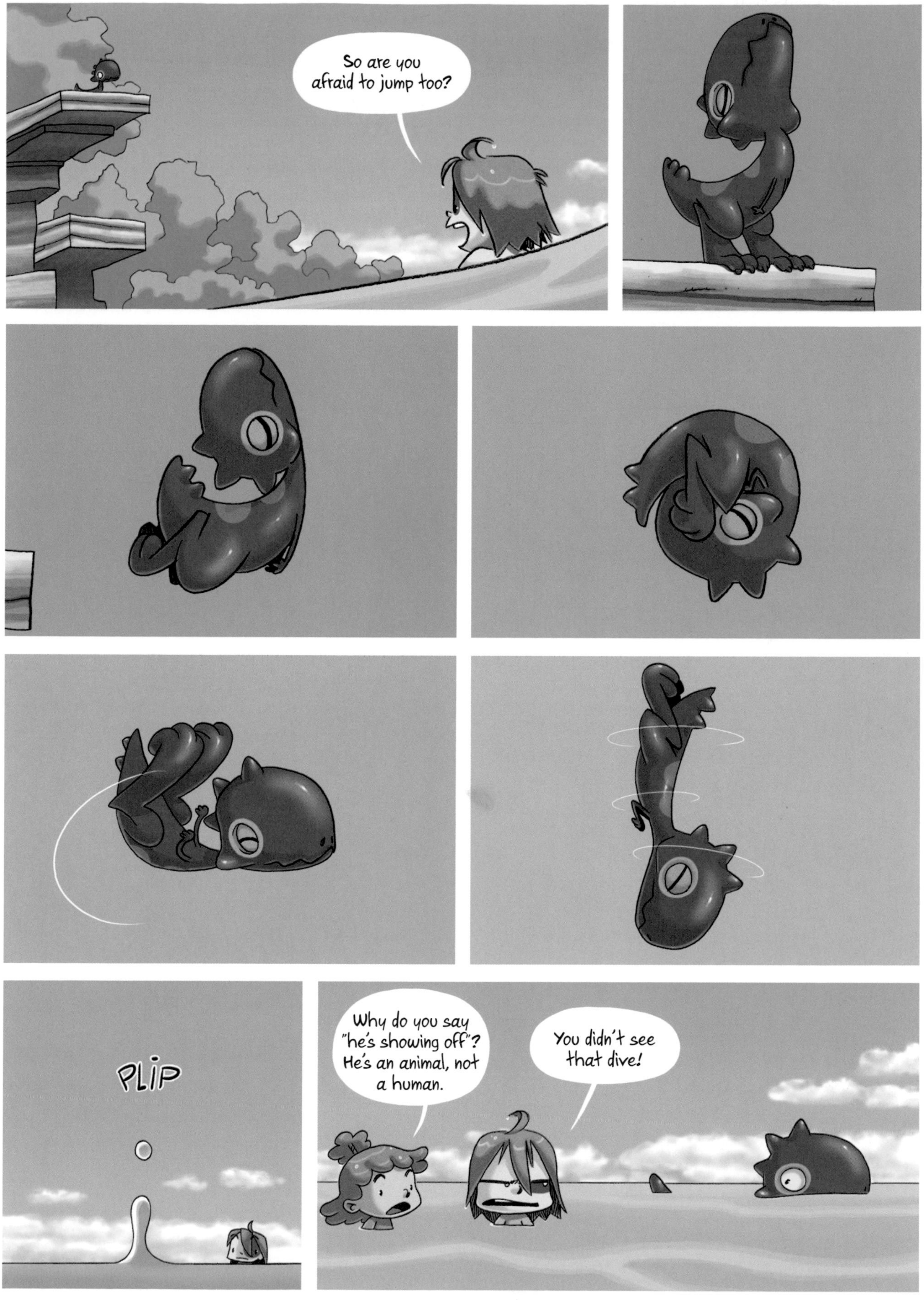
So are you afraid to jump too?
PLIP
Why do you say "he's showing off"? He's an animal, not a human.
You didn't see that dive!

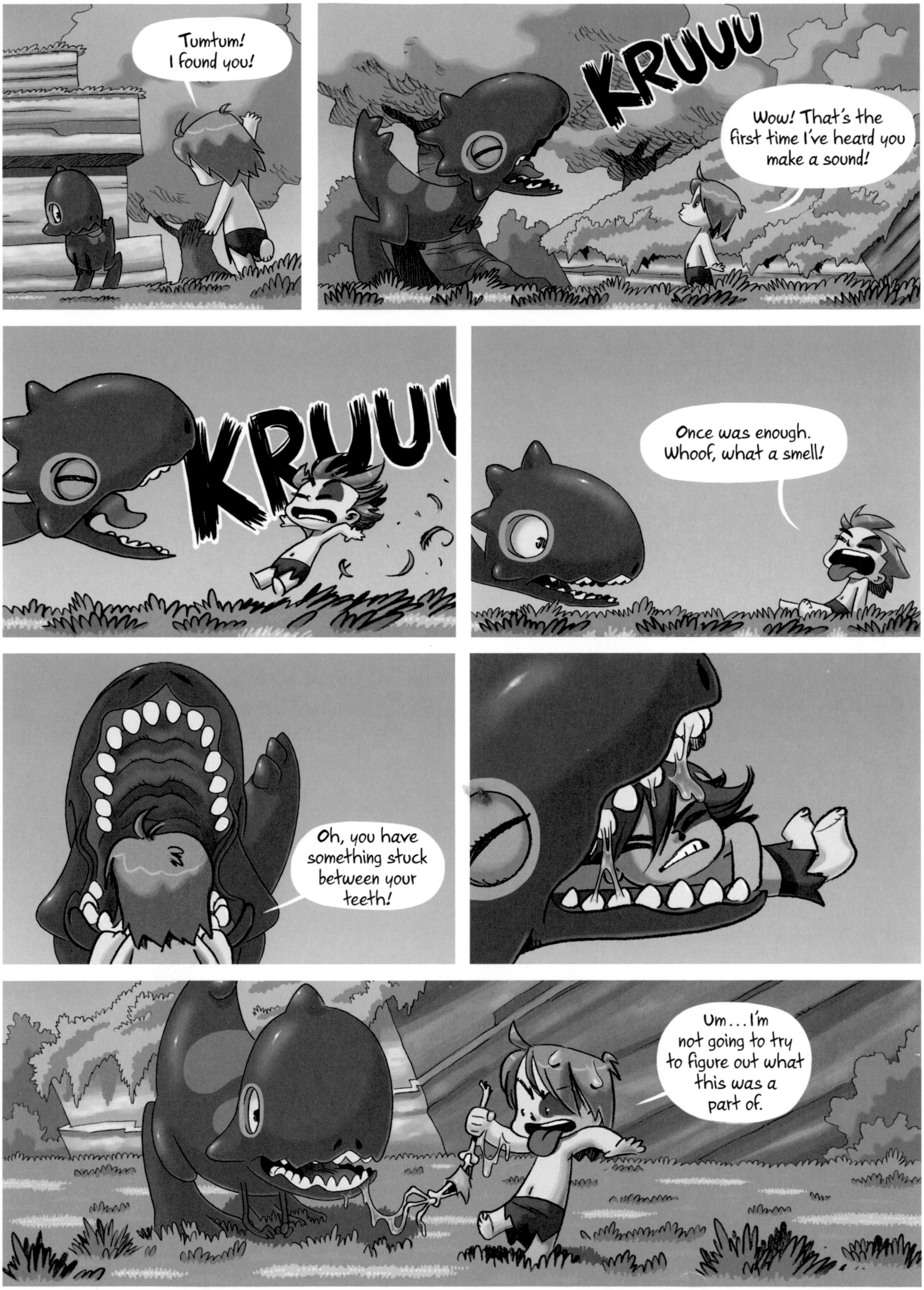

Tumtum! I found you!
KRUUU
Wow! That's the first time I've heard you make a sound!
KRUUU
Once was enough. Whoof, what a smell!
Oh, you have something stuck between your teeth!
Um... I'm not going to try to figure out what this was a part of.

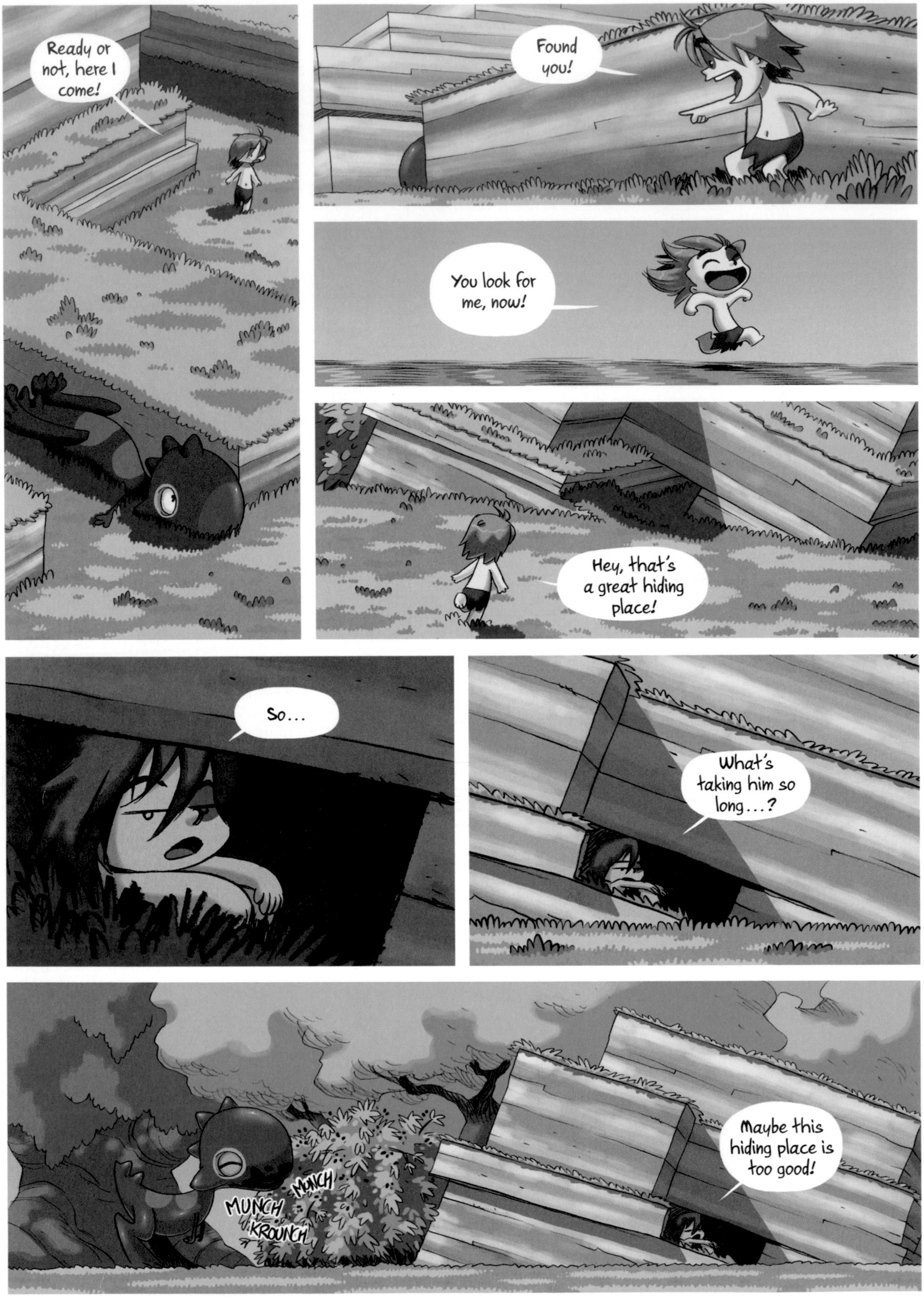
Ready or not, here I come!
Found you!
You look for me, now!
Hey, that's a great hiding place!
So...
What's taking him so long...?
Maybe this hiding place is too good!
MUNCH
MUNCH
KROUNCH

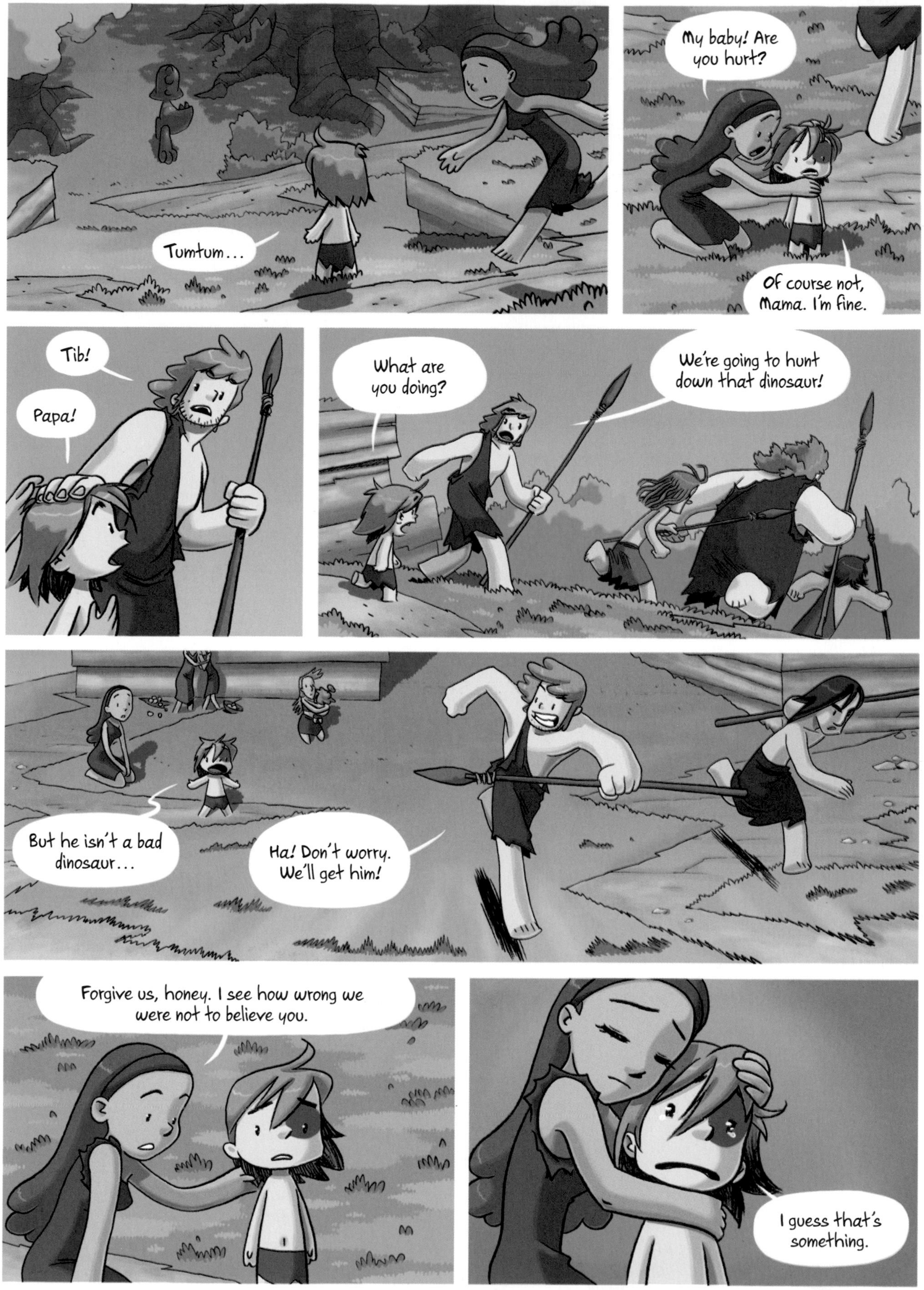
Tumtum...
My baby! Are you hurt?
Of course not, Mama. I'm fine.
Tib!
Papa!
What are you doing?
We're going to hunt down that dinosaur!
But he isn't a bad dinosaur...
Ha! Don't worry. We'll get him!
Forgive us, honey. I see how wrong we were not to believe you.
I guess that's something.

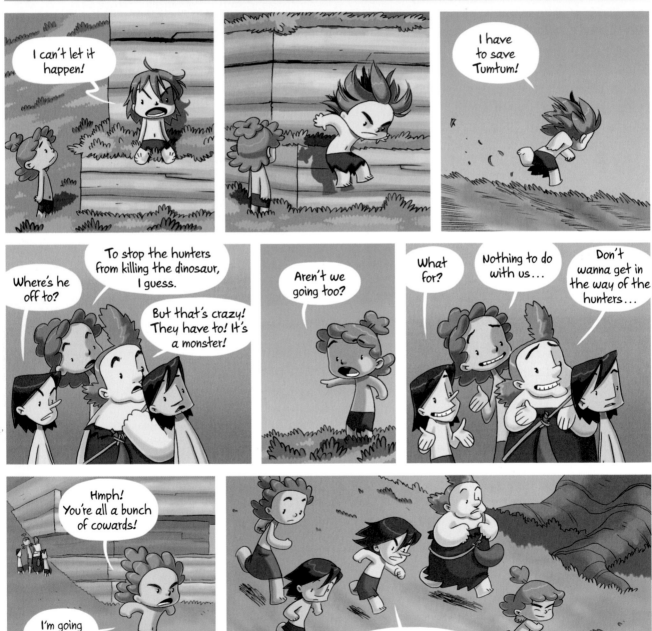

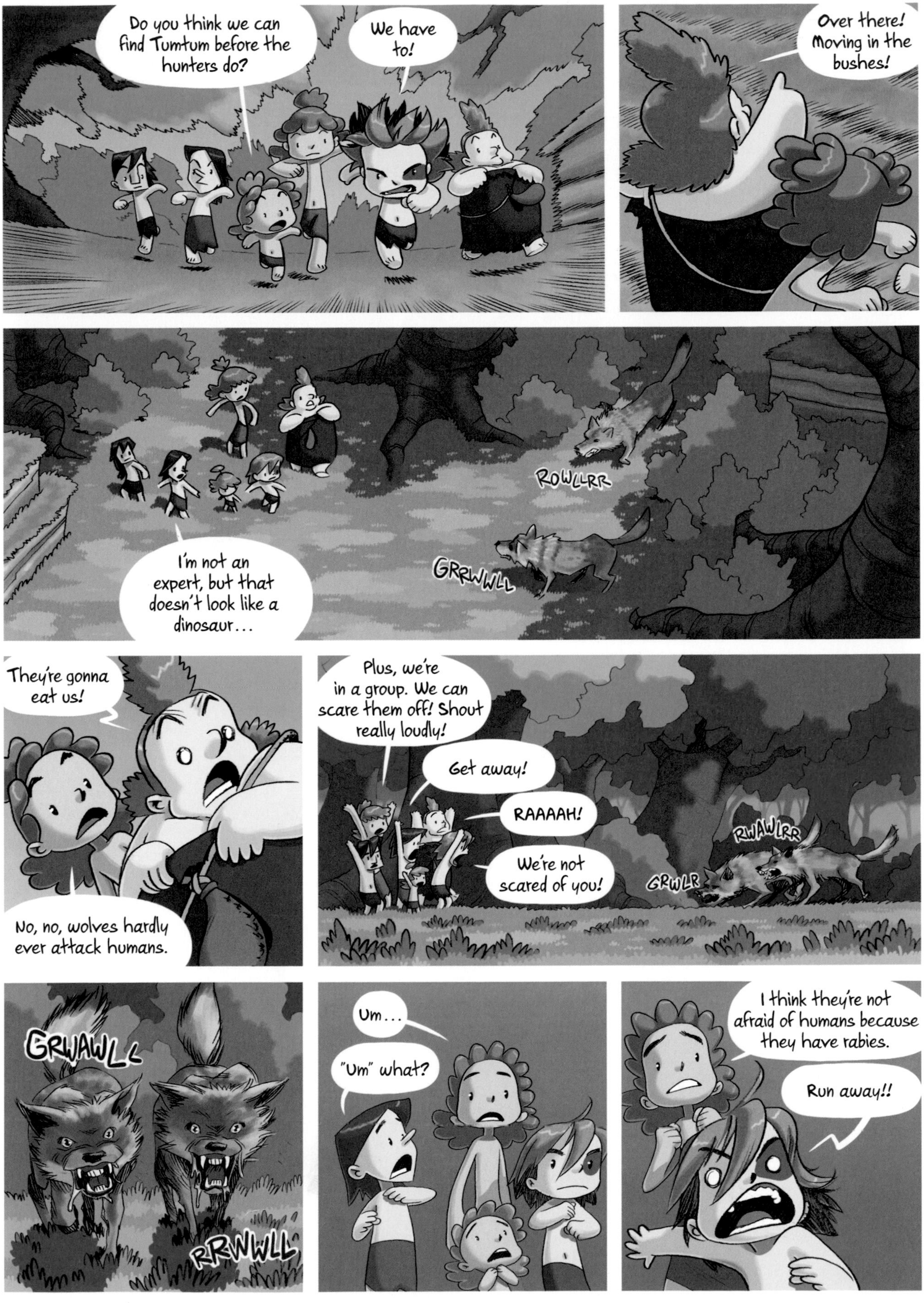
Do you think we can find Tumtum before the hunters do?
We have to!
Over there! Moving in the bushes!
ROWLLRR
GRRWWLL
I'm not an expert, but that doesn't look like a dinosaur...
They're gonna eat us!
No, no, wolves hardly ever attack humans.
Plus, we're in a group. We can scare them off! Shout really loudly!
Get away!
RAAAAH!
We're not scared of you!
RWAWLRR
GRWLR
GRWAWLL
RRWWLL
Um...
"Um" what?
I think they're not afraid of humans because they have rabies.
Run away!!

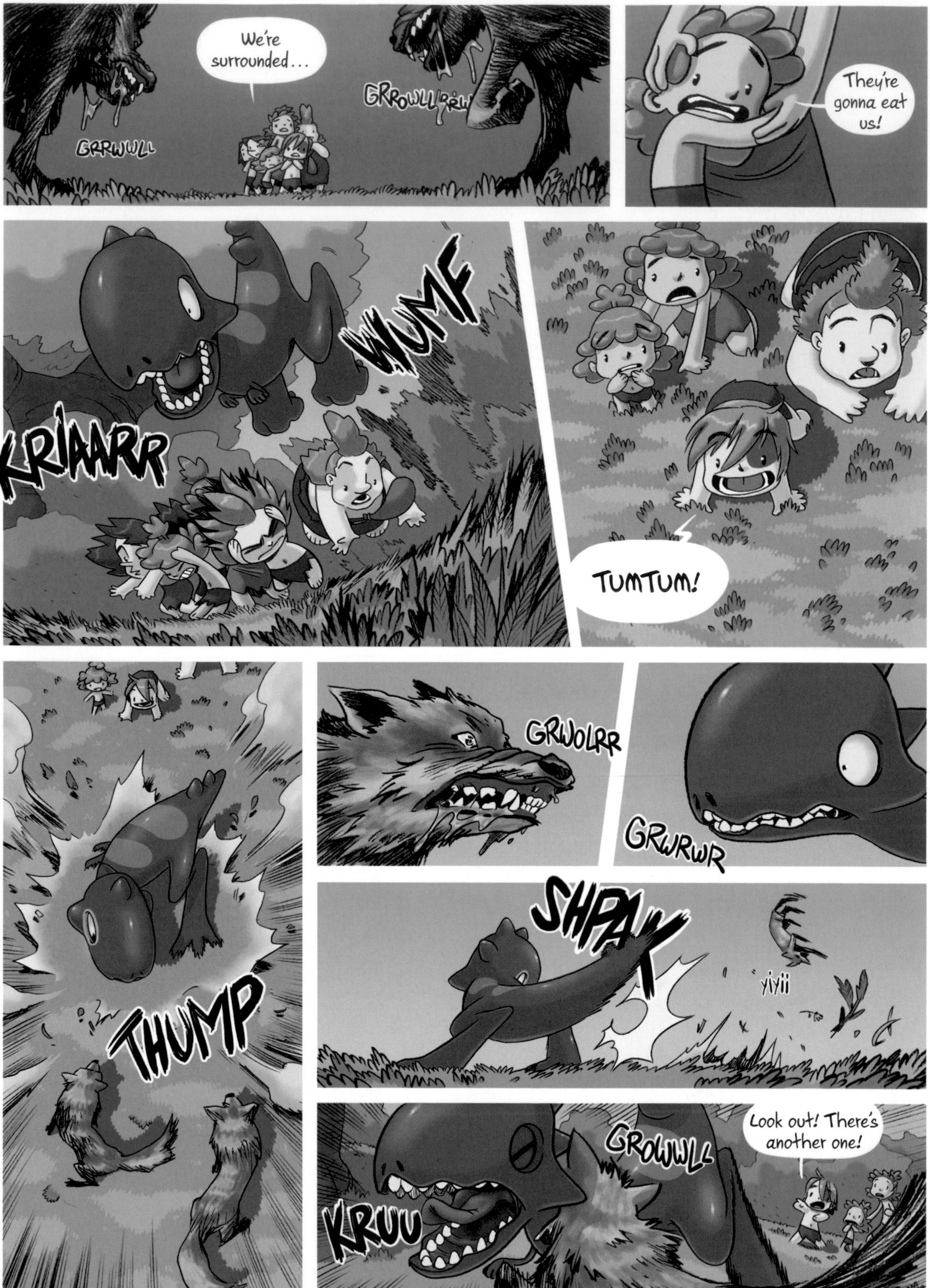

We're surrounded...
GRRWWLL
GRROWLL
GRRW
They're gonna eat us!
KRIAARR
WUMF
TUMTUM!
THUMP
GRWOLRR
GRWRWR
SHPAK
yiyii
GROWWLL
KRUU
Look out! There's another one!

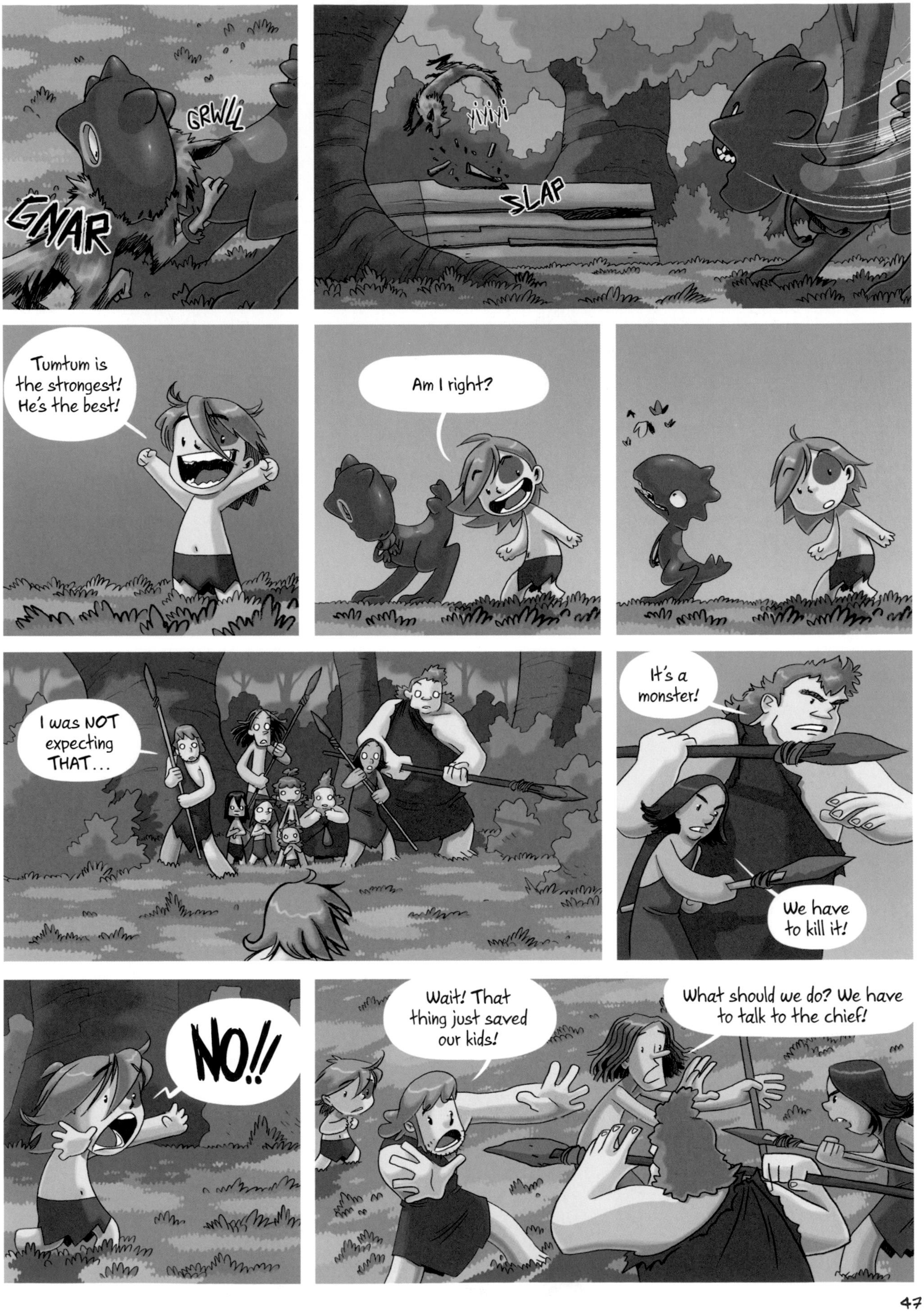
GRWLL
GNAR
YIYIYI
SLAP
Tumtum is the strongest! He's the best!
Am I right?
I was NOT expecting THAT...
It's a monster!
We have to kill it!
NO!!
Wait! That thing just saved our kids!
What should we do? We have to talk to the chief!

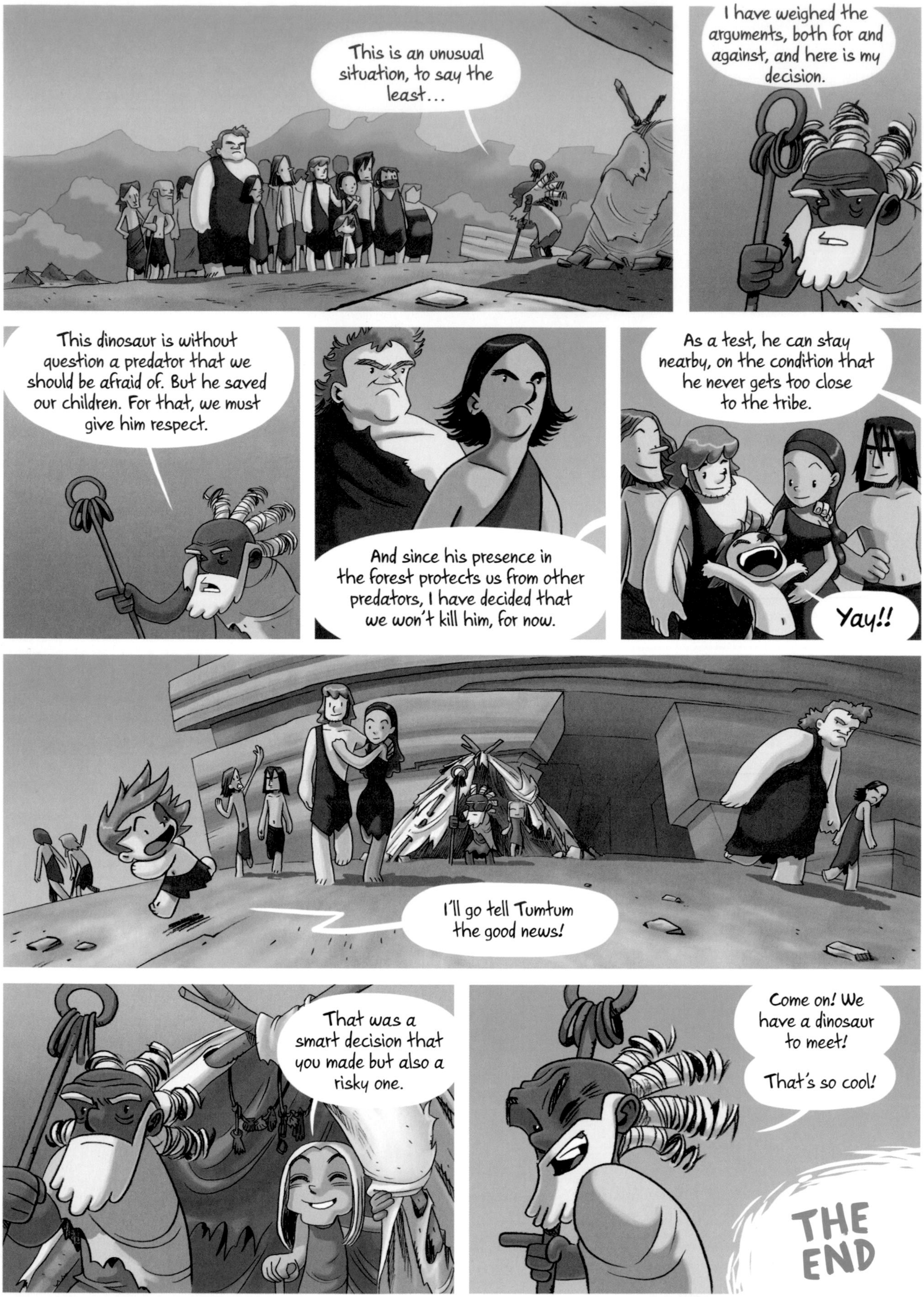
This is an unusual situation, to say the least...
I have weighed the arguments, both for and against, and here is my decision.
This dinosaur is without question a predator that we should be afraid of. But he saved our children. For that, we must give him respect.
And since his presence in the forest protects us from other predators, I have decided that we won't kill him, for now.
As a test, he can stay nearby, on the condition that he never gets too close to the tribe.
Yay!!
I'll go tell Tumtum the good news!
That was a smart decision that you made but also a risky one.
Come on! We have a dinosaur to meet!
That's so cool!
THE END

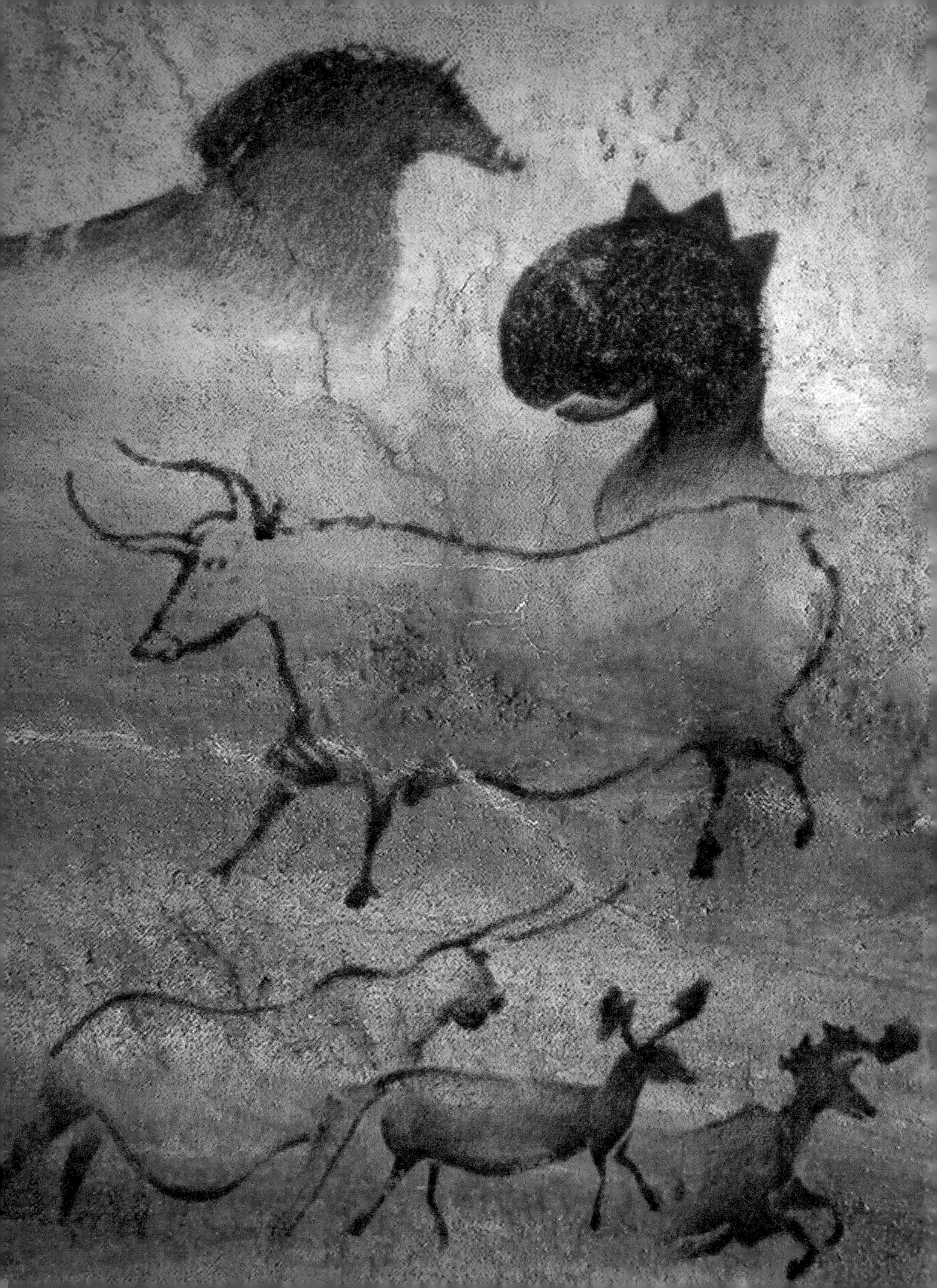